'So, do you fee **asked.**

He shook his head and took Melissa's hand. He wanted to touch her, *needed* to touch her. 'I mean, are satisfied with your job?'

She turned to face him, her mouth quirked up enticingly. 'I think so.'

'Then maybe we should explore other kinds of satisfaction, as well.'

Her breath caught, and she dragged her teeth over her lower lip, the gesture supremely erotic. Kyle's blood heated, and he felt himself harden. The woman turned him on. No question about that.

He stroked her hand languidly, and Melissa closed her eyes, her chest rising and falling as her breath quickened.

'Exactly what kind of satisfaction do you have in mind?' she asked, her voice laced with warm honey.

He didn't say anything, just traced a path to her breast, then cupped the soft weight in his palm.

'As much satisfaction as you can handle, sweetheart,' he whispered.

Dear Reader,

What woman doesn't want a man who'll stand behind her no matter what? That's what I was thinking about when Kyle and Mel introduced themselves to me. And the 'no matter what' was a lot, because Mel just happens to be a cat burglar. And Kyle just happens to be an ultra-sexy former cop who discovers her in his grandmother's bedroom with a very expensive, very stolen diamond necklace.

I thoroughly enjoyed spending time with Mel and Kyle. They both surprised me over and over again, and I hope you enjoy reading their story as much as I enjoyed writing it.

I love to hear from readers. You can visit my website at www.juliekenner.com. If you prefer, write to me at julie@juliekenner.com or at PO Box 151417 Austin, TX 78715-1417, USA.

Happy reading,

Julie Kenner

STOLEN KISSES

by

Julie Kenner

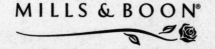
MILLS & BOON®

For Brenda. Thanks, and I owe you a latte.

*First published in Great Britain 2004
by Harlequin Mills & Boon Limited,
Eton House, 18-24 Paradise Road, Richmond, Surrey TW9 1SR*

© Julia Beck Kenner 2004

ISBN 0 263 84035 2

21-1104

*Printed and bound in Spain
by Litografia Rosés S.A., Barcelona*

____Prologue____

EMILY RADLEY SAT ramrod straight in the darkened booth, her posture unmarred despite eighty-six years of gravity taking its toll. Across the table, her longtime friend Gregory Tanner toyed with his drink, not even the slightest bit ill at ease despite the seedy bar and its leather-and-metal-clad patrons.

She'd picked the place because the odds were slim that they'd be recognized at a biker bar just outside of Santa Ana, California. In miles, they hadn't traveled far from their homes near the Orange County beaches, but in California that wasn't necessary to get to a completely different world. As they used to say in the commercials, they'd come a long way, baby. No one would recognize them here. No one in Emily's social circle would come within five miles of the place, much less step inside.

Even Gregory, whose life had overflowed with, well, *color*, wouldn't be recognized. This was the perfect place for their meeting.

Of course, they could have simply met at a Denny's, but the lowbrow nature of the bar had been an additional point in its favor. They'd come here to plot and scheme, and Emily liked the added element of drama that meeting in such a place provided.

She took another sip of her gin and tonic, then clasped her hands on the table. "So we're agreed?"

"I'm here, aren't I?" he said. Even at eighty-five, he still looked as dashing as ever. Once, years ago, Emily'd had a crush on the notorious Mr. Tanner. As a Hollywood ingenue, she'd been unable to pursue it. After all, this had been before the days when being a bad girl got a girl further in the movie business. Now she wondered what she'd missed by not returning Gregory's interest. She'd always had his friendship, of course, but it had been little Martha Kline, God rest her soul, who'd known the secrets of Gregory's heart.

Emily shook her head. It didn't matter. They weren't here about their pasts; they were here about their futures. Their heirs and their families. The two children were simply floundering around, the years ticking away with no one to love or cherish them except a small group of old people. And, as much as Emily would like to live forever, she knew that was one thing her millions could not do for her.

And so Emily and Gregory had contrived a way to bring their grandchildren together, and Emily was absolutely certain that their scheme would work.

Without a word she reached into her purse and pulled out the package. She'd wrapped the jewelry box in brown paper, then tied it with twine. At about six inches long and two inches wide, it looked completely innocuous. Certainly, no one would guess that the contents were worth over half a million dollars.

As he took the package, she noted the way his eyes sparkled. For a moment she wondered if she'd ever see the necklace again, but she quashed the thought. Perhaps foolish, perhaps naive, but she trusted Gregory.

He tucked the package into the pocket of his suit jacket. "Not that I don't appreciate a fine plot, Emily, but maybe we'd be better off simply introducing the kids."

She waved her hand, dismissing the idea. Perhaps they'd been foolish years ago to hide their friendship, but it had been a different era, and it had seemed the best for Martha Kline to keep their contact to a minimum. Now was hardly the time to announce a lifelong alliance, particularly when their grandchildren's ignorance could work in their favor. And, though she'd hardly admit it to Gregory, this way was simply much more fun.

"I've introduced Kyle to so many women he could host a Follies," she finally said. "No. He can smell a setup. We've picked the perfect solution. A situation. A way for them to fall in love without even realizing they're doing it. The perfect script."

"Another Academy Award for your mantel?"

She flashed a camera-ready smile. "I've never won a directing Oscar."

"Well, perhaps this is your year." His gentle smile eased into a frown, and the furrows in his brow deepened. "And Frances is really willing to go along with this charade?"

"Don't act so surprised. We have our differences, of course, but where Kyle is concerned we see eye to eye. The boy needs to settle down." She reached over and patted his hand. "Don't worry, Gregory. We're already halfway through act one, and everything is going smoothly. Kyle thinks I've stolen an heirloom from my sister. And I know my grandson. He's going to try to make it right, and since he's coming to my soiree tomorrow, I'm sure that tomorrow's our night. Everything is falling into place, and now it's time for you to play your part."

"I'm a thief, not an actor."

"Nonsense. You were the most talented and dashing bit player ever to grace the silver screen."

He scowled, his expression turning dubious.

"Don't you dare chicken out on me now, Gregory Tanner. We've concocted the perfect plan. Nothing will go wrong."

For a moment he didn't react. Then he nodded, one efficient motion, and put a twenty on the table to cover their drinks. "I hope you're right. I can't help but think that I've failed Melissa."

"Nonsense. You raised her. Took care of her—"

"Taught her a trade."

Emily sniffed. "How the girl chose to make her living was hardly your doing. The point is that she wishes to be respectable now and you are supporting her wholeheartedly." She stood and he followed suit, then helped her into her coat, a light jacket to ward off the chill from the ocean breeze.

"Still," he said, as she took his arm, "I'm surprised that you consider Melissa suitable for your grandson. Under the circumstances, I mean."

At that, Emily eased closer to his side and tightened her grip on his arm. Then, with impeccable timing, she tilted her head just so, met his eyes, and allowed a mere wisp of a smile to grace her lips. "Of course I have no objections," she said. "I'd be quite a hypocrite if I did."

He studied her face, the lines etched at his eyes finally crinkling into a smile of his own. And right then she knew that he'd seen the hint of desire peeking out from her own countenance, just as she wanted him to. After all, she had two Oscars and three Emmys on her mantel. If she'd wanted to hide her emotions, she was more than capable.

But now, at the twilight of her life and while the two of them were playing with fate...well, this was hardly the time to play the coy shrinking violet. No, this required a much brasher role. And that was a role that Emily Radley had been born to play.

1

A SHAFT OF SUNLIGHT wriggled its way through the east-facing window of Melissa Tanner's bedroom and tickled her eyelashes. She twisted under the sheets, trying to eek out a few more minutes of glorious sleep. One minute, two, she didn't care. She just wanted to float in that wonderful haze between sleep and dreams, that shadowy world where dreams dashed in and out, and where a few more minutes of bliss could be had with just a tap on the snooze button.

"Melissa?" Footsteps sounded on the stairs leading up to her room. "Melissa, you're not going to sleep away the entire day, are you?"

She groaned, pulling the covers up over her head and wishing that one thin quilt could drown out her grandfather's voice. She knew he didn't mean any harm, but was it really necessary to remind her yet again that she was utterly and completely jobless?

His sharp rap on her bedroom door echoed through the room, the sound harmonizing with the sudden high-pitched squeal of her alarm clock. Another seven-minute snooze cycle had passed. Might as well bite the bullet and get up.

"Coming." She tossed the word out in the general vicinity of the door, then sat up, managing in the same motion to swing her feet to the ground.

In the two months since she'd been laid off, she'd crisscrossed Orange County, submitting dozens of résumés and suffering through almost twenty job interviews. She'd had five call-back interviews, but in the end the job always went to someone else. Debts were piling up, property taxes were looming, and her checking account was nearing the two-digit mark.

Not good.

The economy was terrible, and her degree in history wasn't exactly opening doors all over corporate America. If she didn't get a job soon, she was going to be in big trouble. Not only were her savings almost completely gone, she had nothing to fall back on. Not money. Not job skills. Because when push came to shove, except for the one management trainee job she'd so recently lost, she really had no experience that could earn her a living.

Well, that wasn't *entirely* true. She did have one incredibly lucrative set of skills. But cat burglary wasn't a solid career option, and she was determined to be a solid citizen from here on out. Her life so far had been all about secrets, and she was tired of it. Tired of not having any good friends, tired of breaking off relationships after only four dates because she was afraid of getting close. Tired of worrying about getting caught.

Just plain tired. She needed respectability. A real life. A real job.

But unless something changed pretty darn soon, she was going to end up flipping burgers at McDonald's and washing the smell of French fries out of her hair every night.

Not exactly what she'd hoped to be doing at the ripe old age of twenty-four.

No, she corrected herself. Twenty-five. *Happy birthday to me.* With a scowl, she pushed herself off the bed and headed toward the door.

She'd grown up with a grandfather who'd been a living, breathing Robie "The Cat." In *To Catch A Thief,* Cary Grant had ended up with Princess Grace. Well, Mel wanted her own prince, a decent job...the whole fairy-tale life. Was that too much to ask?

"Melissa Jane Tanner, if you don't open this door right now, I'm going to keep your birthday present for myself."

That got her moving. She grabbed the knob and threw open the door. Gramps stood there, looking dapper as always in a linen suit and holding two martini glasses. "A toast," he said, handing one to her as he stepped into the room. "To my favorite granddaughter."

She grinned. "I'm your only granddaughter."

"Then my fondness for you worked out quite well."

With a little shake of her head, she followed as he headed over to perch on the edge of her bed. She took the single wooden folding chair, the only other seating in her tiny bedroom.

She held up the martini. "Let me guess, today you're William Powell from *The Thin Man*."

His face, still ruggedly handsome despite years of wear and tear, lit up. "You always were better at my games than your grandmother or your father."

"The props helped," she said, lifting the martini glass.

"I'll have you know that's a genuine film artifact. I was an extra in *After the Thin Man*. Even met Jimmy Stewart. He was just starting out, you know." She did know, actually. She'd been weaned on classic movies and loved them as much as Gramps did. "My scenes may have ended up on the cutting room floor," he continued. "But at least I got to keep the glasses."

She squinted at the glass, examining it from all sides. "Amazing artisanship," she teased. "But a martini for breakfast? Blech."

"It's your birthday. Anything goes."

Her smile broadened. "I'll keep that in mind."

He waggled a finger in mock warning, but she only laughed. She adored her grandfather and would do just about anything for him.

He was, in fact, the reason that she'd kept doing the cat burglary gig for as long as she had. He'd taken care of her after her parents had died, and as he'd gotten older, it had been her turn to take care of him. The only job she'd known was what he'd taught her, and she'd used those skills to pay the bills, buy the groceries and generally keep them off the streets.

She'd been willing to use those same skills to help fund her college education—a slow process when you had to keep scrambling over rooftops for tuition money. She'd made it, though, and she'd kept the thieving to a minimum. And now that she was legit with her shiny bachelor's degree on her wall, she didn't intend to return to a life of crime.

But unless she could figure out a way to pay those property taxes, she might have no choice. Because the one thing she wanted even less than returning to that life was seeing the house sold out from under them. Not only was this house all she had left of her parents, but it was the home she shared with Gramps. She wasn't giving it up. No matter what.

She knew a lot of girls her age might balk at living under the same roof as their grandfather, but Mel had lost her parents in the blink of an eye. One of these days Gramps would go, too, and she wanted to have shared as much as possible with him before then.

"And one more toast," he said, lifting his glass. "To new beginnings and bright futures."

"I'll drink to that," she said, "especially if by 'bright' you don't mean under the fluorescent lights of some fast-food restaurant."

"I don't, indeed." He took a sip of his drink, and she did the same, then immediately spit it out, unable to swallow through the burst of laughter.

"Gramps! This is *water*."

"Well, of course, Melissa. I'm certainly not going to imbibe before the cocktail hour."

She rolled her eyes, and then, just to show him, she slammed back the rest of her drink, then fixed him with her best stare. "Personally, I like my mineral water shaken, not stirred."

He shook his head. "James Bond. Really, Melissa, you're not even challenging me. Can't you come up with a more obscure film?"

"Not in my jammies, I can't." Besides, at the moment she wasn't feeling particularly sharp. For that matter, lately she'd been feeling like quite a loser. After all, how hard could it be, *really*, to find a job?

Apparently, it was pretty damn hard.

"What?"

She scowled. The man knew her too well. "I'm just wondering what I bothered with all that school for. I mean, it took me forever to finish my bachelor's, and for what? So I can pound the pavement looking for a job that's not there?"

"You'll find one," he said. "You already did. You had a perfectly fine position at that rental agency."

"Perfectly fine until I got laid off." Budget cuts, and she'd been the first to go. The downside of being low on the totem pole.

The sad truth, though, was that she'd secretly rejoiced the day she'd gotten her pink slip. The job had been duller than dull, and she'd taken Gramps all the way into Los Angeles for a fabulous dinner, just to celebrate her freedom.

At the time, she'd assumed the job would be easily replaceable. Little did she know.

What she *did* know was that she couldn't continue as a cat burglar. It was too risky. Too illegal. It simply wasn't right. Even more, she hated living a constant lie.

But could she help the fact that no other job offered the thrill she got from inching her way into someone's locked room? Pathetic, she knew, and she'd turned over a new leaf. Melissa Tanner had gone straight as an arrow. If she got the urge, she'd take up bungee jumping. But cat burglary was off-limits. Totally and completely.

Gramps stood and crossed the room to her desk. He put his glass down and turned to face her, his gaze serious.

"Grandpa?"

"Maybe it's time for you to give up the pretense."

She swallowed, afraid he was going to call her out, accuse her of *wanting* to be a thief. "The pretense?" she repeated, hoping she sounded innocent.

"The job situation," he said. "Why don't you simply take some time off while you evaluate your options and figure out what you need to do?"

A lovely idea, but hardly practical unless he was going to suggest thieving as a way to pay her bills. And she knew he wouldn't do that in a million years. Gramps knew better than anyone the perils and pitfalls of a life of crime, and he'd pushed her out of the profession with all the force he could muster. The only other time he'd shown such determination had been when he'd taught her the skills that had kept her from ever getting caught.

"Gramps, I appreciate the thought, but even if I could convince the county that they don't need those silly old taxes, we still have food and a car payment and other expenses."

She hated laying it out like that, especially when she knew that Gramps had no money to help her out with. He'd long ago run through his savings, and social security didn't make payments to retired thieves.

She sighed. "I just need to find a job. Since I've already run through all the usual channels, I'm thinking I'll try to find something that has a little kick to it. Maybe the Parks Service. I mean, that has to be interesting. Or maybe at one of the amusement parks. Adventure. Excitement. My cup of tea, right?"

"I'm sure you would get immense job satisfaction out of running a cotton candy machine, but before you make a new career plan, at least take a look at my birthday present to you."

"It wasn't a watered-down martini?" A weak joke, but it was the best she could do under the circumstances. Without reason, a finger of dread had begun to tickle the back of her neck, and she wondered what Gramps was up to. He'd always talked about wishing he could help her be more financially independent. But surely he wouldn't have gone and done something stupid. Would he?

He reached into his inner jacket pocket and pulled out a black velvet jewel box tied with a red satin bow. Mel's heart skipped a beat as she took the box from him. *Oh, dear Lord, he would.*

She tried to keep her fingers from trembling as she tugged the bow free, then carefully lifted the hinged lid. Inside, snuggled in the black velvet lining, lay the most beautiful diamond necklace she'd ever seen. And, frankly, she'd seen quite a few.

Oh no, oh no, oh no.

She lifted the necklace, her practiced eye examining the stones, her stomach twisting as she took in the high quality of the diamonds and the incredible workmanship. The necklace had to cost around half a mil, and that meant that this was bad. This was very, very bad.

She looked at him, her expression surely reflecting both fear and disbelief. She didn't even try to hide it.

"Oh, Gramps," she said, her voice barely a whisper. "What have you gotten us into now?"

DIAMONDS MIGHT BE a girl's best friend, but right then both diamonds and women were giving Kyle Radley no end of trouble.

He stood next to an oversize buffet in his grandmother's living room as the din of fifty or sixty voices surrounded him, bouncing off the marble and polished wood, seeping under the Chippendale chairs, and creeping behind the French tapestries hanging on the walls. He ignored them all, concentrating instead on coming up with a solution that didn't involve stealing a five-hundred-thousand-dollar necklace from his grandmother.

Nothing. He couldn't come up with one single alternative.

If he wanted to keep Miss Emily out of trouble—not an easy task—he was just going to have to buckle down and swipe the necklace. Right now. Tonight. Before it was too late.

Even though he'd seen it with his own two eyes, he still couldn't quite believe she'd stolen from her own sister. And not a trinket. No sir. At a family gathering last week, she'd hauled away a diamond necklace that would have felt right at home among the crown jewels.

Kyle had witnessed the event, and his former-cop instincts had kicked in. He'd confronted his grandmother right then and there, but she'd refused to return the thing, citing a sisterly right to the necklace that Frances had apparently inherited from their father. Kyle didn't remember any family stories about the piece, but he was hardly in a position to challenge Emily's memory. Not when she had the necklace tucked into her brassiere, and Frances's jewelry box was conspicuously empty.

Frances might be a sweet old thing to Kyle, but she was also the *numero uno* threat to Miss Emily's role as the Empress of Emerald Cliffs. The two sisters had a long-standing feud that even their shared devotion to Kyle couldn't seem to reconcile. Where social status was concerned, family loyalty meant nothing, and when Frances realized Emily had swiped her necklace, Kyle knew she'd call the cops faster than Miss Emily could line up a blind date for him.

In retrospect, he probably should have simply told Frances and let the chips fall where they may. After all, someone needed to teach Miss Emily that she couldn't have every little thing she wanted in life. But considering she was pushing ninety, it seemed a little late for that lesson, and besides, did he really want his grandmother frisked and finger-printed at her age?

No, he didn't. And so he'd wimped out, deciding instead to simply grab the necklace and return it to Frances's house himself. With any luck, he'd get it back before his aunt even realized it was gone.

His grandmother would be furious, but he'd face her wrath when he had to.

Right then the woman in question was holding court across the room, silver-gray hair piled on her head, a shocking-purple gown clinging to a figure that still made heads turn. Only, now it wasn't because of her curves, but because...well, because she was Emily Radley. The self-appointed social direc-tor of Emerald Cliffs and the nearby communities along the Pacific Coast Highway.

A crowd of a dozen senior citizens gathered around her as she regaled them with tales from her studio days. He could hear only the high points as words like "Garbo," "Mayer," and "those fabulous Technicolor musicals" drifted by on the floral-scented air.

He'd been reared on her stories, and he loved every one of them. Out of habit, he started to drift in that direction, but he caught himself and stopped. Not only did he need to take advantage of the opportunity to sneak upstairs, but he also didn't want her to notice him. Lately Miss Emily's conversations with him were touching less on her old movie days and more on his love life. So far she hadn't used the party as an excuse to play matchmaker. He'd almost asked her if she felt ill, but had decided not to press his luck.

And her silence really *was* luck. He may have worked for ten years as a Los Angeles cop, getting down and dirty with the south-central gangs, but the horrors he'd seen didn't even come close to rivaling Miss Emily's guerrilla tactics where his love life was concerned. He didn't know how long the respite would last, but he was grateful for it, though he feared she was simply planning her secondary campaign.

Abigail Van Martin, his grandmother's best friend and his self-appointed great-godmother, marched toward him, her cane more of a prop than a necessity. "Kyle, darling, you shouldn't be here."

"I know." He ran his fingers through his hair, causing Abby to frown. When he was eight, she would have smoothed the hairs back into place. Today, thankfully, she kept her hands to herself. "I should be at work. I've been at work all day. I've been busting my tail trying to solve this Driskell mess."

Kyle had retired from the force to open his own security consulting company, Integrated Security Systems, and for the first year things had been going great. Then Ethan Driskell had purchased Integrated's top-of-the-line burglar alarm system, and three weeks later thieves had wiped him out, the value of their haul totaling over nine million dollars.

For Driskell, a millionaire several times over, the theft was serious but not devastating. For Kyle it was a public-relations disaster. He needed to find the flaw and find it fast, before word got around and his growing client list shrank to nothingness.

So, yes, he needed to be at the office rather than standing around at his grandmother's party. But Miss Emily's antics had sucked him in, and he was here for the duration.

Abby squinted at him, her glasses hanging from a chain around her neck. "Driskell?" She shook her head, confused. "I meant why are you *here*? In the corner. You should be out circulating. Meeting the young ladies."

Kyle couldn't help but laugh. His entire business could be collapsing around his ears, and Abby and Emily would only wonder if he had a date for the event. "I knew it was too good to last. Grandmother's gone the entire party without mentioning my pathetic bachelor state. Don't tell me she enlisted you as the second guard."

Abby sniffed. "I was simply making an observation. But your grandmother is right."

He stifled a sigh, half wondering if he should invent a girlfriend and short-circuit the old ladies' campaign altogether. The idea amused him, especially since it held an irony his grandmother was eventually sure to see. How many times had she told him the story of her fake fiancé, created by the studio to make her seem that much more desirable when the "wedding" fell through?

Abby tapped him on the foot with the tip of her cane, snatching his attention back. "You're such a good-looking boy. When are you going to settle down?"

"Come on, Abby. Don't tease me. How can I think about settling down when I can't find a woman half as nice as you?"

"Save your charm for the younger ladies, dear." She patted his cheek. "I prefer a wrinkle or two in my men. Makes me feel like we're even."

"Give me a few years."

"Don't tempt me." She fumbled for the glasses hanging from her neck, then pushed the specs onto her nose and squinted at him. "Have you been looking for one?"

"One what?"

"A woman, dear. Do pay attention."

He chuckled. He should have known Abby Van Martin wouldn't beat around the bush. "Honestly? I haven't been looking at all." His priority right now was saving his business, not getting laid.

At that particular moment, though, neither his floundering business nor women were the issue. Diamonds were.

He bent down and pressed a quick kiss to Abby's cheek, then made his excuses, telling her he was off to circulate with the female party guests.

It wasn't true, of course.

But he could hardly explain to his godmother that he was heading upstairs to break into his grandmother's wall safe and steal a diamond necklace.

MEL SCRAMBLED UP the ivy-covered trellis, then eased over the balcony railing. She moved silently back toward the wall, slipping into the shadows, then looked around, checking for prying eyes.

Nothing.

She exhaled. So far, so good.

Usually she prepared more for a job, but with this

one she'd had less than a day of prep time. She closed her eyes, drawing a deep breath as she forced herself to relax, forced her heart rate back to normal.

Hard to believe that mere hours had passed since Gramps had given her the necklace, confessing that he'd lifted it from the wall safe of Emily Radley, one of Hollywood's early stars.

She still couldn't believe he'd done something so foolish. Overlarge gemstones were too hard to fence, and Gramps didn't believe in taking unnecessary risks.

This time, though, he'd taken it for her. To secure her future.

She was pissed and touched all at the same time, and it had taken every ounce of strength in her body to reject the gift. He'd been so proud of himself, and she'd trampled all over him. She'd seen the desolation in his eyes, and she'd rushed to tell him how much she appreciated the thought, not to mention the risk. He'd been out of the game even longer than she had, but for her he'd rushed back in, pell-mell.

"And what if you'd been caught?" she'd said.

"Did you forget who trained you? Have *you* ever been caught?"

He knew, of course, that she hadn't.

"It's not a question of getting caught," she'd said, trying a new tactic. "The point is, I'm trying to go clean. Responsible. A new leaf. How can I start a new life if I'm financing it with Miss Emily's stolen necklace?''

He'd sighed, a heavy, world-weary sound. ''If it means that much to you, then I'll return the necklace.''

''Good. It means that much.''

''Fine. I'll just buy you a blender for your birthday. Or perhaps a Barnes & Noble gift certificate.''

Mel had rolled her eyes, then stood up and crossed to the bed to kiss his cheek. She'd sat next to him, the mattress sinking under her weight as she'd squeezed his hand, still clutching the jewelry box in her free one.

''Why on earth did you steal from Emily Radley?''

Gramps had looked confused. ''What do you mean?''

''Well, doesn't she know you? I mean, you had minor roles in at least a dozen of her movies.''

''Ah. Yes. Well, that's true. I suppose we were somewhat acquainted.''

She'd rubbed her temples. ''Gramps, your reputation as some mysterious cat burglar might have made you a romantic figure back in the forties, but nowadays she would've just called the cops.''

''You're right, you're right. You're absolutely right.''

She hadn't expected such quick agreement and

decided not to press the point. "Tell me about Emily's house."

He had. Describing the very balcony on which she now stood, the trellis he'd climbed just a week before and the bedroom that he'd navigated to find the necklace. The thought made her queasy. Dear Lord, what if he'd fallen and broken his neck?

"*I'll* return it," she'd said. And she hadn't been willing to entertain any arguments.

Now, as she stood on the balcony, she realized for the first time that he hadn't actually *made* any arguments. Instead he'd simply nodded his head, looking a bit like a scolded puppy, as he'd proceeded to describe the best way into Miss Emily's mansion.

"And you should go tonight," he'd added. "According to this morning's paper, Miss Emily is having a party. She always shuts her alarm system off while the festivities are going on."

"And you know this how?"

He'd looked affronted.

She'd waved the question away. "Never mind. You did your homework. Fine. I'll go tonight."

And now here she was, standing on a darkened balcony outside Emily Radley's bedroom, a half-million-dollar necklace in her fanny pack along with various tools of the trade.

It was a ridiculous, inconvenient, annoying situation, and the hell of it was she hadn't felt such a rush in the past eight months.

She was back in the game and she was enjoying it to the max.

Considering she'd officially retired the day she'd graduated, the trill of excitement in her blood was a very bad sign indeed.

Below her, little electric torches lined the circular driveway, their flickering light causing the shadows to dance across the balcony. She tried to stay in the dark, but it was difficult, and she hoped that no one would step outside and look up. If they did, hopefully the black stretch denim jeans and black turtleneck T-shirt would keep her unseen in the shadows.

Careful to avoid big movements, she tested the doorknob, the latex gloves she'd slipped on before entering the grounds ensuring that she wouldn't leave any telltale fingerprints.

Locked.

A minor setback, but hardly insurmountable. She could pick the lock. And, if she couldn't, she had contact paper and glass cutters in the fanny pack. She pulled out a set of picks and set to work. One minute…three…five…

Damn. One more try, and if she didn't get it, she was going to have to go through the glass. She guided in the pin, twisted, and—

Success.

The tumblers fell into place and the lock turned. Thank goodness.

She slipped inside and automatically moved away from the doorway, then braced for the squeal of an alarm, even though Gramps had sworn that Emily would have disarmed the thing. When fifteen seconds passed without an ear-splitting screech, she finally relaxed, then scanned the moonlit room, letting her eyes adjust as she took in the ornate furniture, the canopied bed, the overstuffed armchairs and the cherry wood vanity.

An antique mirror in a gilded frame hung on the far wall, and she headed in that direction, certain the safe was behind the heavy frame. She peeked under the corner and, sure enough, there it was.

Taking care, she lifted the heavy frame, revealing the metal face of a standard, somewhat old-fashioned, wall safe. She shook her head, quelling the urge to make a *tsk-tsk* noise. Really, you'd think superrich people would keep their jewelry in state-of-the-art safes, not some old dinosaur that she could access without even breaking a sweat.

Working fast, she opened her fanny pack and removed an instrument that helped her as she felt for the hesitations that marked the numbers of the combination. She'd figured them out in about five minutes, took another six minutes to get the order correct, then dialed in the correct combination.

Click. The tumblers fell into place, and she pulled the safe's door open.

Just like riding a bicycle.

Black velvet boxes filled the safe, some open, others still closed. Items of jewelry peeked out, strands of pearls tangled with diamond bracelets...sapphires gleaming in the low light...rubies sparkling like sin.

It took every ounce of willpower she possessed not to poke through the pile, pulling out and examining each exquisite piece. She'd always had a passion for jewelry—it tended to go along with the profession—and this was like being a kid loose in a candy store.

No time.

Right. She needed to get moving. Forcing herself back to the task at hand, she unzipped the fanny pack and pulled out the necklace, its facets seeming to catch even the tiny bit of light that had filtered into the dim room.

No doubt about it—the necklace was exquisite. She'd seen some amazing pieces of jewelry during her career, but this necklace was truly the pièce de résistance. Warm and inviting, the necklace seemed to call to her, begging for her touch. Just one simple little caress. Just one moment of playing the princess.

No. Absolutely not. Very bad idea.

The necklace sparkled in the streams of moon-light, twinkling out Morse code. Dot, dot, *do* it. Dash, dash, *try* it.

No, no, *no.*

Before she could change her mind, she pulled the jewelry box from her back pocket, placed the neck-lace inside and snapped the lid shut. Then she shoved the box into the safe, slammed the door, and spun the dial.

Done.

Thank goodness.

For just a moment, she stared at the closed safe, her latex-covered fingertip tracing the line of her neck. She stifled a sigh, already regretting not trying on the necklace. After all, how many more times would she have such an opportunity?

Never, right? Because she was out of the business. This was it. Her one final chance to feel fire and ice kiss the curve of her neck.

She licked her lips. Maybe it wouldn't hurt to—

Click! The sound echoed through the room.

Mel stiffened, heart racing, as she tried to locate the cause. Silence. Maybe just house noises? Echoes from the party two stories below?

Maybe you should put that mirror back and get the hell out of here.

Right-o. She hefted the mirror, managing with surprisingly little effort to hang it back in place. She adjusted it, then backed up, trying to see if she'd managed to hang it straight.

And that's when she stepped on it. Hard, yet malleable, like a lump of leather.

She crunched her heel down and felt whatever it was give just a little. How odd. It felt almost like—

"Would you please get off my foot?"

A shoe.

2

MEL FROZE, thrown off-kilter by the owner of the shoe's deep, rich voice. Then slowly, carefully, she inched sideways toward the French doors and away from the shoe—and the man attached to it.

"Hello?" That voice again. Surely the owner of such a melodic voice wouldn't trundle her off to jail. "You want to turn around so I'm not talking to your ponytail?"

"Um, no. Actually, that's not my first choice." She was perfectly content to stand there staring toward the balcony. Longing for the balcony, actually.

"Humor me," he said, and there was no denying the command in his voice.

With a little sigh, she reached up, her fingers closing over her ponytail holder. She knew she was playing a dangerous game, but she needed to buy time and she really didn't see any other alternative. She sure as hell didn't need a B&E on her record, not when she'd gone her whole career without even an arrest. No, right now she was willing to do pretty much anything to get out of there without getting the cops involved. And if that meant turning on the charm, well, then that's exactly what she intended to do. After all, Gramps had been in over a dozen movies. Surely she'd inherited *some* acting ability.

She tugged on the band and the thick, chaotic hair that annoyed her so much sprang free, falling to the middle of her back. She flipped it, taking care to make the gesture as sultry as she could without actually turning around to face him. "There," she murmured. "Now you're not staring at my ponytail."

"Not exactly what I meant," he said, his voice closer now.

"No?" A hand closed on her shoulder and spun her around. "I—" She tilted her head back, ready to kick the flirting into overdrive, but stopped short, all rational thought evaporating.

Gorgeous. Absolutely, positively, one-hundred-percent knock-your-socks-off, take-your-breath-away gorgeous. Sandy-blond hair. Rich-blue eyes that were crinkled at the corners with a combination of amusement and irritation. Broad shoulders and a trim waist accented by a dress shirt and tailored slacks.

Forget pretending to flirt, a man this fabulous deserved the real thing, a wonderfully flirty turn of phrase that would ensure he not only let her go but also feel madly, hopelessly under her spell. But her head was in too much of a muddle to produce even a coherent sentence.

"Who the hell are you?" he demanded.

The bubble burst, and Mel straightened, feeling stupid. She'd lost herself in the fantasy, allowing the rush of adrenaline from the whole necklace caper to color her perception about everything, including this man. This *stranger*. But this wasn't a movie, he wasn't her leading man, and she needed to concentrate if she wanted to get out of there with her reputation—and her record—intact.

With supreme effort, she forced herself to play it cool, then conjured a slow smile. "I'm nobody important." His hand still rested on her shoulder, and she fought a rush of awareness. Whether she wanted to or not, her body was determined to notice this man. However, she was equally determined to keep tight control over the situation. As much as she could, anyway, considering she'd been the one caught in the wrong place at the wrong time.

She lifted her chin and met his gaze. "Maybe we can keep this our little secret?" In desperation, she actually batted her eyelashes.

"Our secret?" He frowned, his hand moving from her shoulder as his fingertip traced a path down her arm. It was everything she could do not to shiver. "Yeah. Maybe we can."

"Really?" She cleared her throat, forcing her body back into a more casual, self-assured posture. She had no idea why he was willing to back off, but she wasn't about to argue. Her grandfather didn't raise a fool.

"I think so," he said. "As long as you're clean."

She cocked an eyebrow. *"Excuse me?"*

"Arms wide. Legs apart."

She stared down her nose, trying to gauge if he was serious. Apparently, he was. She did a quick calculation, decided there was no way she'd survive if she took a running leap toward the balcony, and assumed the stance.

His hands skimmed over her, a purely professional pat down, but there was nothing at all professional about the heat generated by his touch. He did a quick press under the curve of her breasts, and she bit the inside of her cheek, trying to will her nipples not to peak. The situation might be completely humiliating, but with this man running the show it was damned enticing, as well.

She closed her eyes and started counting backward from fifty, hoping the mindless activity would distract her. It worked until twenty-five. That's when his hands skimmed up the inside of her thighs. She jumped, then scooted away from his touch. "Okay, okay," she said. "That's just about enough of that."

The corner of his mouth twitched, but he didn't argue. Instead he said, "Nice gloves," then pointed to her fanny pack. "Open it."

She did, and he poked through the contents.

"Quite the collection of tools," he said. "Want to tell me why you're here?"

"No."

He nodded. "Okay. Then maybe you want to tell me why you broke in only to look at a diamond necklace and then put it right back where you got it?"

"You saw me?"

"I walked in as you were putting it back in the safe."

"And the pat down was to make sure I hadn't taken anything before you walked in?"

"Smart girl."

"No."

He frowned. "No what?"

"Your earlier question. No, I don't want to tell you what I was doing."

"You're one of those UC Irvine students, right?"

She had graduated from UC Irvine, but she still had no idea what he was talking about. "What makes you say that?"

He ran his fingers through his hair, giving him a sexy, tousled appearance. "Oh, come on. It's been all over the paper. Upping the ante. Dare after dare. Basic college pranks on steroids. It's dumb."

She nodded, trying to look scolded. "Yeah. You're right. It is." She casually lifted one shoulder. "Uh, sorry?"

He exhaled, and she wondered if he was going to change his mind and call the cops. Or maybe the dean of students. Time to short-circuit this little tête-à-tête and get the heck out of there. "Well, this has been a real treat, but I really should be heading out."

He studied her, and as his gaze rose, so did the heat in her body, oozing up her legs, her stomach, her breasts, until she felt she might spontaneously combust. Then his lips curved into a smile. The kind of smile that said, "You can't fool me," but a smile nonetheless. Maybe she amused him. Shaharazad managed 1001 nights just for keeping the king amused, and got to stay alive in the process.

Maybe his grin was a good sign.

Or maybe she'd lost her grip on reality.

All in all, she really didn't have the upper hand in this little scenario.

He stood right in front of her, and though he was only a head or so taller, he seemed to loom over her, one giant wall of masculinity. She swallowed and held her ground, but it was all she could do not to step back, to claim her space again. He had a presence, a compelling strength, and her pulse had picked up tempo simply from his proximity.

What on earth was coming over her? She stood straighter, taking deep, even breaths as she forced herself back to the moment. The real moment. The one where she'd been caught breaking and entering. Not the fantasy moment where the gorgeous, sophisticated man discovered her inner charm and whisked her away from "all that."

After a moment he broke eye contact, stepping back toward the door that led into Miss Emily's hall. His hand closed over the doorknob. "There's no sense risking your neck on the trellis," he said. "I'll show you to the servants' stairs. You can get out through the back door."

She tilted her head and squinted at him, certain that at any moment a big, orange Warning! sign would start flashing over his head. As much as she wanted to get the hell out of there, something in her gut was telling her this just wasn't right.

"You're really just going to escort me to the stairs? That's it? No interrogation? No bright light shining in my eyes? No water torture or hypodermics of sodium Pentothal?"

He shrugged. "Sorry. Not today."

She squinted. "Why?"

"You seem like a nice girl."

"I am. Yes. But—"

"Well, there you go. Just try to avoid hanging out with the wrong crowd at school."

He waved his hand toward the door in a hurry-up gesture, and, just like that, she *knew*. He wasn't supposed to be in that room any more than she was. He was too eager for her to leave, too lackadaisical about her presence in the first place.

Had he come for the necklace? She didn't know, but she didn't intend to leave until she found out. She'd worked her tail off to return the thing to Emily, and she'd be damned if she was going to stand by and let this charlatan with the bedroom eyes rip the old lady off.

Besides, now that she was pretty certain he wouldn't turn her in, this was becoming a fun little escapade. And, on the whole, a hell of a lot safer than bungee jumping.

Her mind made up, she took a seat on Miss Emily's plush divan, then crossed her legs for effect. "Actually," she said, conjuring a smile, "I think I'm going to stay awhile."

KYLE RAKED HIS FINGERS through his hair and considered just picking up the slip of a woman and tossing her out on her rump. He decided against it. For one, manhandling women tended to be frowned upon. For another, he had no idea what she was up to. When he'd first seen her, his heart had raced, certain that she'd violated Miss Emily's sanctuary. His pat-down had proved otherwise, though. Unfortunately, the pat-down had made his heart race for an entirely different reason.

He told himself that he'd been eager to clear her out the room so he could get down to business, but that was a big fat stinker of a lie. No, he'd tried to rush her out of the room because he found her so damn distracting.

Considering the way she filled out those tight black jeans, he'd lay money that any male with a pulse would have reacted just like him. Because this little thief was one fine-looking woman. Stunning, really, her big green eyes staring up at him in the dark, with equal parts of contrived innocence and defiance.

He tried to ignore the irony. Ten thousand women his grandmother had thrown at him, and the only woman he'd ever found attractive was a feisty little gal he'd caught in a compromising position. He had no clue what that said about his character, but at the moment he didn't care. He'd watched, silent, as she'd tucked the necklace into its box and then stashed it in the safe. She'd broken in, yes. But she hadn't stolen. His pat-down had confirmed that.

So what exactly was she up to?

He didn't really believe the UC Irvine story; she'd jumped too eagerly onto the explanation. But the truth didn't matter right then. At the moment he had another agenda on his mind, and unless he missed his guess, he figured he had less than fifteen minutes before Emily came looking for him.

He didn't have any choice. Company or not, it was time to move the process along. He turned back to the safe, then dialed in the combination he'd known since his teenage years. The door swung open and he took out the jewel box that he'd watched Emily pilfer from Frances's bedroom. He opened the lid, confirmed the necklace really was inside, then slipped the box into his jacket pocket. Tomorrow he'd change the locks on Emily's balcony door and see to it that she kept her alarm armed even during parties.

He headed toward the door. "Come on," he said, trying to sound casual as he tossed the words over his shoulder. "We're leaving through here."

"'Come on?' she repeated. "*Come on?* You're just leaving? Like that? With the necklace?"

"Well, I could have you arrested for breaking and entering, but considering you didn't steal anything, I think the cops would probably just have a good laugh and let you go. Hardly seems worth my effort." Okay, that wasn't the least bit true, but it sounded good. And he sure as hell didn't want to get the cops involved. If Frances ever caught the scent of what Emily had done, she'd hound the cops until they had no choice but to press charges against his grandmother.

"So you're just going to let me go?"

"That's what it comes down to."

She glared. "*You're* the one stealing a necklace." She pointed an accusing finger toward his pocket.

"Where the hell do you think you're going with that?"

"I'm returning it," he said, "to its owner."

She paled, and Kyle didn't have to be a genius to realize he'd struck a nerve. "Okay," he said. "Spill it."

"What do you mean by 'its owner'? Isn't that Miss Emily's necklace?" She pointed vaguely in the direction of his pocket.

"It belongs to Frances McIntyre."

"Who?"

"Emily's sister."

"Oh." Her brow furrowed. "No, that can't be right."

"Trust me. It's right."

She squinted at him. "Prove it."

"Sure," he said. "No problem." He hoped his voice conveyed more confidence than he felt, because he had absolutely no idea if he could prove it or not. His only hope was the engrained family habit of labeling everything. Their father had been a farm worker, and Emily, Frances and their parents had moved from camp to camp. According to Emily, the two girls had learned to write their name on anything. If they didn't, any one of the other camp children would simply acquire it, and the girls' belongings would soon dwindle to nothing.

He pulled the box from his pocket, keeping his fingers mentally crossed. Then he opened the case, revealing the stunning necklace. He didn't waste time enjoying the view, though. Instead he turned the piece over, his eyes going automatically to the clasp. When he saw it, a smile bloomed on his mouth, and he held the necklace out to the girl.

"Looks like I win, sweetheart. I think maybe it's time I show you to the door."

She leaned in closer, then scowled at the "F" and "M" engraved on the flat clasp. "How do I know you're returning the necklace?" she finally asked. "For all I know you could be stealing it."

He stared at her for a moment, measuring. Then he dug into his pocket and pulled out his tiny little cell phone. He tossed it at her, impressed when she caught it with one hand. "Report me."

He held his breath, praying she didn't call his bluff.

She held the phone like a worry stone, her thumb rubbing its silver back. "I thought *I* was returning the necklace," she finally said. "To its owner." She met his eyes. "To Emily."

He shook his head. "Returning it? You mean you came here *with* the necklace?"

She nodded, and he exhaled. That would teach him to jump to conclusions. He hadn't actually believed the UC Irvine story, but he'd still assumed she was some sort of thrill seeker who just wanted to see if she could get into Emily's bedroom and safe. But if she'd been *returning* the necklace, that raised a whole host of new questions. "So you lied," he said. "You're not a student."

She shrugged. "Sorry. Character flaw."

He rubbed his temple. "So then what's the real story? And no BS this time. Where'd you get the necklace, and why did you bring it back?"

"Just being a Good Samaritan."

"Why don't I believe that?"

"Maybe you have trust issues?"

He ignored that. "Well, someone seriously misinformed you about where to bring the necklace. It belongs to Frances, and that's where I'm taking it right now."

"And I'm just supposed to believe you? For all I know you're heading out that door to pawn the thing."

He raised an eyebrow but kept silent, waiting to see what she'd say next. He knew she'd say something. He hadn't spent countless hours interrogating suspects without internalizing a few tricks of the trade.

But she didn't say anything, and for a moment he thought he'd met his match. When she finally broke, he had to give her credit for being one tough customer. Not many people could keep their mouth shut for so long in the face of a gaping silence.

"Look, buddy. You're not supposed to be in this room any more than I am. And there's no way I'm letting you out of here with that necklace."

"I'd say I have a little more authority than you."

"Yeah?" She lifted her chin, and he had to admit he found the defiance utterly sexy. She didn't have a leg to stand on and she was still arguing her point. In any other situation, with any other woman, he'd find the gesture obstinate as hell. But this woman got under his skin. Which was a simple fact that he didn't intend to examine too closely. He had enough on his plate right now without figuring out how to squeeze a sexy little burglar into the mix.

"Okay," she continued. "Prove it."

"My name's Kyle Radley. Emily's my grandmother. Frances is my great-aunt."

"Oh." She blinked, and he thought he'd scored a

victory. She'd leave, and he could get on with his life. "So what?"

He exhaled. So much for counting his chickens. "So, this is a family matter. I appreciate that you brought the necklace here. Now I'll get it back to its rightful owner."

"Sorry, bucko. Whatever you're selling, I'm not buying."

"Excuse me?"

"I'm getting this necklace back where it belongs, and that's not in your pocket. I don't care whose grandson or nephew you are."

"I told you. I'm *returning* the necklace. To my great-aunt."

"So you said. But how do I know it's true? You still might be trying to steal the necklace. Do you have any idea how many major thefts occur among relatives?"

As a matter of fact, he did. A lot. He kept his mouth shut.

"You say it belongs to Frances," she continued. "Fine. I'll believe you. But it either stays here with Emily or I see it end up with Frances." She cocked her head. "You ever see *Raiders of the Lost Ark?*"

"Of course." He was too startled by the non sequitur to do anything but answer.

"Until I see that necklace find its way home, it looks like you've got yourself a partner." She smiled. "And I'm sticking to you like glue, mister."

MEL PUT HER HANDS ON HER HIPS, determined not to let this guy out of her sight until that necklace was safe and sound with either Emily or Frances.

He might really be a relative, but she didn't trust him any further than she could throw him, and if he snatched the necklace, then Gramps was going to be up a creek. The cops might never realize he stole it in the first place, but she couldn't bank on that. She needed everything squared away if she wanted to sleep at night without worrying about her grandfather.

Besides, she wanted to go straight, and how could she really have a clean conscience unless she knew for certain that he hadn't pocketed the thing? She couldn't.

Which meant that she intended to stay right by his side until he kept his word. Half a mil provided a lot of temptation. And although Kyle Radley might be gorgeous as sin, it was the "sin" part that concerned her. She'd known some pretty sexy con artists and thieves in her time. And she'd learned the hard way not to trust a pretty face.

"All right," she said, when his continued silence started to grate on her nerves. "Let's get going." She peeled off her latex gloves and shoved them into her fanny pack.

"I don't think so."

She lifted a brow in a gesture that she hoped was regal. "I don't recall making that a question."

He studied her, and she pulled herself up to her full height, all five feet six inches, determined to make absolutely clear that she didn't intend to broach any argument. "I told you. You're not getting rid of me. Get used to the idea."

Apparently, either her words or her body language worked, because he finally gave one curt nod. "Fine. It's not worth arguing about. We'll go in the morning."

She put a hand on her hip. "Oh, right. Like I'm going to let you slip away for eight hours. We go now."

"It's after midnight. No."

She exhaled. "Why the hell not? She's got a butler, right? Just call ahead, we go over, give the necklace to him, we go home."

"Frances doesn't know the necklace is missing. And I don't want her to."

Well, she couldn't argue with that. "So we go

now, sneak inside, put the necklace back and get the hell out."

"She's got a state-of-the-art alarm system. I installed it myself."

She almost asked him what he meant by that, then realized it didn't matter. "I can get around it."

He shook his head. "I don't think so."

She crossed her arms over her chest and lifted her chin. "Wanna bet?"

"The morning," he said. He took her by the elbow and steered her toward the door. "We'll go first thing in the morning."

She squinted at him. "And in the meantime? We're just going to hang out here until morning?"

"Not here," he said. "But we are going to be spending the night together." His smile broadened and she saw amusement dancing in those deep-blue eyes. "It's a long time until morning." He took a step closer, and her pulse picked up tempo, his proximity firing her senses.

He reached out, curled one strand of hair around his finger. "So tell me, sweetheart. Got any ideas about how we might pass the time?"

3

MEL DREW IN A BREATH and willed her body not to react to his touch. She knew he was simply trying to get a rise out of her, and she didn't intend to give him the satisfaction.

Instead she was determined to match him measure for measure. She held out her hand and waited for him to take it. His fingers were firm and warm against hers, and when he gave a tiny squeeze she met his eyes.

Time to head out into the world. Or at least out into the rest of the house.

"I'm going to try to sneak us out. Just act casual. And if anyone sees us, let me do the talking."

She nodded. That was fine with her, although she frantically hoped no one would see them. She wasn't wearing a sign that said, Hey, I'm a Thief! But neither was she dressed for one of Emily's social occasions, either.

He pulled open the door, then led her into the hallway of a house that rivaled any of those dumps Robin Leach showed off. From Emily's bedroom on the third story, they headed down an impressive staircase with an ornately carved banister. Soft jazz and muted voices wafted up from the first floor. For just a moment, Mel imagined herself on a dance floor, twirling to the music, Kyle's arms tight around her.

She shook her head, cursing her own stupid romanticism. He was putting up with her because she'd foisted herself on him. That was all. Nothing more. And as soon as the necklace was safe and sound in Frances's house, she'd probably never see Kyle Radley again.

And that, she told herself, was a good thing.

When they reached the second level, he splayed his hand across her back and steered her to the far side of the stairway. "Stay to the back," he whispered. "We're going to try and cut over to the service stairs without anyone down there noticing."

Fine by her. They took a few tentative steps in that direction, and just when Mel was certain they were home free, she heard footsteps on the stairs below. Kyle muttered a curse, and Mel knew that they'd been caught.

She clutched his hand tighter. He might not be her knight in shining armor, but at the moment he was the best she had.

Below them, Emily Radley glided across the second-floor landing. *The* Emily Radley. Former goddess of the silver screen and star of at least five of Mel's absolute favorite classic movies. She'd known all along whose house she was in, of course. But until she was actually seeing Emily Radley in the flesh, the truth of her surroundings hadn't fully hit home.

Emily looked up and did a little Queen's wave. "Kyle, darling. There you are. I've been looking everywhere for you."

"Sorry, Grandma," he said, leading them down the stairs toward Emily. "I had to help out a friend."

"Sorry about my attire," Mel said, desperate for the woman to know she didn't always dress like this. "My, uh, car broke down near here, and I called Kyle on his cell phone and..." She trailed off, realizing she had no clue where to go from there.

"I'm so sorry about your car troubles, Me—my dear." She took Mel's hand and squeezed, the gesture both friendly and supportive. "And you look perfectly lovely. Black is a very 'in' color."

Mel just nodded, unable to completely comprehend that a fashion maven had just given her jeans a thumbs-up.

Miss Emily focused on Kyle, still keeping Mel's hand in hers. "Did you ring Turner?"

"I can handle it, Grandma."

"Turner?" Mel couldn't help her curiosity. Kyle glared at her, but she just shrugged.

"My chauffeur. He's a mechanic, too, of course."

"I think I'm capable of changing a flat tire," Kyle said.

Miss Emily let go of Mel just long enough to pat Kyle's cheek. "Of course you are, darling." She turned back to Mel. "I thought I knew all of Kyle's friends. You are...?"

"Very pleased to meet you," Mel said. She wasn't about to give her real name, and now she scrambled to think of a fake one before Miss Emily asked her point blank.

"Grandma, meet my friend Grace," Kyle said, while Mel gaped at him. *Grace?* Where the heck did that come from? "Grace, my grandmother, Emily Radley."

Emily cupped Mel's hand in her own, then patted her knuckles. "It's a pleasure to meet you, Grace. Have you two known each other long?"

"Not really. You could say we stumbled across each other and just sort of hit it off." She turned to Kyle, keeping her eyes wide and innocent. "Wouldn't you say?"

"That about sums it up." He gripped her arm, his fingers tightening just above her elbow. As he pulled her back, Miss Emily tugged her forward.

She felt like a tug-of-war rope, and she yanked hard, tugging her arm free from Kyle, all the while aiming a stern glare in his direction.

He glared right back. "We really need to get going," he said.

"Oh, darlings, that's such a pity. Can't you even stay for one drink? Surely Grace's car will wait."

"No, we—"

"That would be great," Mel said, interrupting. "We'd love to have one drink."

Kyle scowled, but Mel just shrugged. She *did* want to stay. She adored Emily Radley and under other circumstances she'd have given anything to be at one of her parties. Considering she'd never have the chance again, she might as well grab the opportunity and run with it.

"We really should get your tire changed," Kyle said, speaking slowly and distinctly, as if she were chronically stupid.

"Don't be silly," she said. "The car's not going anywhere." She lifted an eyebrow. "Besides, I don't have anyplace in particular to be until morning."

With that, of course, she knew she'd won that battle.

And then, while he seethed, she flashed him her most innocent smile, knowing full well that right then he probably wanted to kill her.

HE WANTED TO KILL HER.

What the hell was she doing? He was trying to escape and she was tossing them both right smack into the lion's den.

The woman was obviously delusional. Didn't she realize that there were at least a dozen women down there determined to meddle in his love life? They were going to think she was the flavor of the week, and that was something he really didn't want to deal with.

Frowning, he followed Emily and Grace-the-mystery-woman down the stairs, and Kyle watched her move in step with his grandmother. She was graceful, athletic, with a slim waist and a firm rear. One arm was linked through Miss Emily's as she carefully helped the older woman down the stairs.

Kyle rolled his eyes. Their guest might be a thief, but Miss Emily was a con artist. She no more needed help maneuvering those stairs than an Olympic gymnast needed help walking a balance beam.

"Now, Grace," said Emily, as the women took another step down, "have we met?"

Grace looked back over her shoulder at him, a tentative smile on her mouth. "No. I haven't had the pleasure."

"Funny," Emily said. "You just look so familiar to

me." She patted Grace's arm. "Doesn't matter. We've met now."

The women continued to chatter on—Kyle was frankly amazed that the girl knew so much about his grandmother—until they reached the ballroom. Emily caught the eye of the bandleader and lifted one finger. On cue, the orchestra began to play *Kiss Me Quick, Melissa,* and Grace clapped her hands, almost bouncing with the music.

"Oh, my gosh! This is my favorite song. My grandfather and I used to dance to it when I was a little girl." She turned to Emily with such excitement in her eyes that Kyle couldn't help but smile. "And you were fabulous as Melissa. *Stolen Kisses* is one of my all-time favorite movies."

"It's one of my favorites, too," Emily said. "I taught Kyle how to dance to this tune. Remember, dear?"

He grinned. "Oh, yes. I remember it well." Actually, those dance lessons were one of his fondest memories. Though, frankly, all of the summers he'd spent with his grandmother had been special. A cherished respite from traipsing all over the globe with his diplomat parents.

As the women beamed, he held out a hand for his grandmother. "For old-time's sake," he said.

But she didn't take his hand. Instead, she pressed

Grace's hand into his and then gave her a tiny push into his arms. "Not old times," she said. "New memories. Show Grace what a wonderful dancer you are."

He opened his mouth to protest, but the feel of the woman in his arms stayed his tongue. He did want to dance with her; at the moment, there was nothing else he'd rather do. And so he guided her to the floor, counting out time with the music as they twirled under the twinkling lights of the crystal chandelier.

He closed his eyes, letting the melody carry them. Simply dancing.

"Where'd you get Grace?" she finally asked.

"*To Catch A Thief*," he said simply.

"Oh." A pause, then. "That's one of my favorite movies."

"Mine, too," he admitted.

They danced a few minutes more in silence.

"Thank you," she whispered, her soft voice tickling his ear.

"For what?"

"For letting us come down here. For dancing." She shrugged in his arms. "I mean, to be here. To meet your grandmother. I know you wanted to go, but—"

"Hush," he said, unable to help his smile. One

moment she was tough as nails, the next she was a starstruck fan. Damn, but she amused the hell out of him. "I'm not mad anymore. Just stay quiet, listen to the music, and maybe I'll forget I ever was."

She nodded, stiff at first, but then she relaxed, her body molding to his, her head resting on his shoulder. And as they glided over the dance floor Kyle let himself forget that he didn't even know this woman, this thief. That his grandmother had ripped off his great-aunt. And that his business was about to crash and burn.

No, right then all he wanted was to hold her, to feel her soft curves move against him and hear her little sighs of pleasure. She was vibrant and alive, and Kyle felt as if he'd stolen a little piece of heaven.

And for as long as the song continued, he wasn't about to give it back.

"Yes, yes," Emily said, whispering as she spoke into the phone. She was making the three-way call in the alcove just off the ballroom. She peered out toward the couple. "They're here right now."

"And you think the plan is working?" Frances asked. "Already?"

"They're *dancing*," Emily said, unable to keep the excitement from her voice. "And they look quite cozy."

"Of course it's working," Gregory said, his voice firm on the line. "I never doubted Emily for a second."

"I almost called her Melissa," Emily confessed.

"For Pete's sake, Em," Frances blurted. "Don't screw this up for us."

Emily bit back her retort. For the sake of the kids she could be civil to her sister. "I'll be careful," she promised. "And you should expect them later on."

"In the middle of the night? Surely not. Kyle has better manners than to wake me."

"Wake you?" That was Gregory, sounding more than a little miffed. "My Melissa can get into your house without even breaking a sweat."

"We're sure she can," Emily said, playing peacemaker. "But since Frances will be retiring soon, it doesn't matter. Frances, dear, check your jewelry box the minute you get up and let us know if they've returned the necklace."

"Roger," Frances said, and Emily pictured her saluting.

"Anything else to report?" Gregory asked.

Emily considered telling him about Melissa's revelation about the song. She could even picture him, all dapper and refined, letting a little girl stand on his polished shoes so he could teach her to dance.

But in the end, she kept the image to herself, tucked away in her heart.

"That's it," she said instead. "Here's to success."

They repeated the rallying cry and then clicked off.

And Emily went back into the ballroom to attend to her guests.

"NOW HOW DID YOU TWO MEET?"

"It's so nice to know that Kyle has a young lady friend."

"And what do you do, dear?"

Mel's glance bobbed from woman to woman as their comments swirled around her, becoming little more than a static-filled buzz in her ear. She'd been in heaven in his arms, ecstatic when she'd become a guest at a real Emily Radley party.

Now, though, she saw the downside. The reason why Kyle had wanted to skip the party and head straight out the backdoor.

These women had an agenda, and as far as she could tell, she was now on the menu as a possible dish for Kyle.

He'd known, of course, that the women were going to circle and attack. And that's why he'd abandoned her after their dance. Payback.

She smiled politely at the women, grateful none

had yet noticed that she was entirely avoiding their questions.

She raised her gaze over the sea of gray-and-blue-haired heads and caught his eye, hoping her expression conveyed that he needed to get his rear back over there. Right that second.

He held up a glass of champagne as though to ask, "Want some?" She sighed, then nodded. Champagne. Wine. Straight Scotch. Anything to help get through this little ordeal.

The truth was, under normal circumstances, she might actually be enjoying this. After being raised by Gram and Gramps, she got along famously with the senior citizen set. But these were not normal circumstances.

"Are you and Kyle dating, dear?"

She started to concoct an answer, but fortunately the man himself eased up beside her and handed her a drink. Then he took her free hand and twined his fingers through hers. It was a casual gesture, but right then it seemed anything but. Not when his fingers were pressed against hers, firm but gentle. And not when he was looking down at her with that crooked smile and those dreamy eyes.

"Now, Abby," he said, sliding smoothly into the conversation. "You know I'm not dating anyone in particular right now."

Mel found herself almost sagging with relief from that tidbit of information. *Ridiculous.*

The bespectacled woman just smiled and tapped the tip of her cane on the parquet floor in front of him. "I can hope."

"Ladies," he said, hooking his arm through hers. "I'm afraid Grace and I really do need to get going."

Finally! "It was nice meeting all of you."

They said a few more goodbyes as they made their way to the front hall. Emily met them there and gave them each a quick kiss. "It was lovely to meet you, Grace. Now that we've met, please don't be a stranger."

"Thank you," Mel said. *Emily Radley* told her not to be a stranger. Oh, Gramps was not going to believe this.

Finally they were out the door. A valet in a white coat with red epaulets trotted over to take a ticket from Kyle, then he jogged off into the dark.

"A valet?"

"My grandmother likes to go all out when she throws a party."

"I guess so." She licked her lips. "So, uh, thank you."

"For what this time?"

"For getting us out of there."

"Notice how I'm not saying 'I told you so'?"

She scowled. "You're lucky I'm not chewing you out. You threw me to the wolves, you know."

"Hell, yes."

"Thanks a lot."

"Sorry," he said, sounding anything but. "I guess I just assumed you could think on your feet."

At that, she just glared.

"Right," he said, amusement dancing in his eyes. "You're a thief, not a con artist. Got it."

She opened her mouth to retort, then thought better of it, focusing instead on her fingernails. Not surprisingly, she was unable to find a nail with anything left to nibble. She shoved her hands in her pockets.

When the car arrived, she wasn't sure if she was disappointed or relieved. It was your basic So Cal transportation, a Jeep Grand Cherokee. A fabulous vehicle—certainly out of her league—but considering who his grandmother was, Mel had been expecting something more ostentatious. A Ferrari, perhaps. Or a bright-red HumVee.

"The limo's in the shop," he said.

Her cheeks warmed, and she kept quiet, the fact that he once again had read her so well more than a little disconcerting.

She climbed in, buckled up and didn't say another word as he maneuvered the broad curves of the Pacific Coast Highway. Once or twice she sneaked a glance in his direction and decided that her first impression didn't do him justice. Kyle Radley was more than just gorgeous. He was like ambrosia for the eyes. Absolutely perfect to look at, and, she had to admit, the man was perfectly nice as well. That, of course, scored him major bonus points. Especially since she knew damn well that if he really wanted to get rid of her he could.

She'd said she was sticking to him like glue, but it was one o'clock in the morning, the highway was deserted, and he had a good seventy pounds on her. If he pulled over and dumped her at the side of the road, there was no way she'd win that battle.

The thought gave her pause and she sneaked another sideways glance. As far as she could tell, he wasn't about to toss her overboard.

Good. She told herself she was simply interested in seeing that the necklace made it back to its rightful owner. She feared, however, that she was telling herself lies.

They turned off the highway and headed into a small neighborhood just behind BJ's Pizza in Laguna Beach. A couple more turns and he pulled in front of a charming bungalow with a perfectly manicured front lawn. About a million times smaller than Emily's place. But what it lacked in size, it made up for in warmth.

"Home sweet home," he said.

"I love it." She meant it, and when she stepped inside, she loved it even more. The house was bigger than it looked, and seemed to go on forever. The floors were hardwood, the walls sparkling white. The effect would have been austere were it not for the warm furnishings and paintings. Overall, the place was homey. Mel liked it immediately.

"Come on," he said, and she followed him toward the kitchen. "You hungry?"

She realized then that she was. "Starved."

He gestured toward the table. "Take a load off." Then he opened the refrigerator, made a disgusted noise, and popped his head back out. "So, uh, how do you feel about cereal?"

She fought a smile. "Has the milk expired?"

"Three days to go. We're safe. I've got Cap'n Crunch, Cheerios, or All Bran."

"Any one of those is great."

"Good." He sounded relieved. He plunked the three boxes onto the table, then got them bowls, spoons and the milk. She poured herself a bowl of Cap'n Crunch and dug in.

"Considering how much I just slaved to feed you, don't you think you owe me the rest of the story?"

"No."

"If there's someone out there stealing from my grandmother, I think I have a right to know."

He probably had a point, and she took another bite of cereal while she considered what to do. Then she told him the story. Or, at least, she told him the highlights. Frankly, her honesty surprised her. But why not tell him? He already knew the basics, and it wasn't as if there was anything between them. Even if they were to have a wild, torrid affair, it wouldn't last. It couldn't. He already knew too much.

"So, your grandfather stole the necklace from Emily and gave it to you?"

She shrugged. "Retirement fund." She made a face. "*He's* supposed to be retired, too. I can't believe he pulled a stunt like this just for me."

He took her hand then, his eyes warm. "Are you that hard up for cash?"

She concentrated on the tabletop, ignoring the way he was drawing lazy circles on her palm. Heat formed under his touch, and she fought the urge to rip her hand away, both terrified and fascinated by the reaction he caused in her body.

"Grace?"

Mel stared at her palm. Her toes were tingling. His touch had sent a ribbon of heat through her body that literally warmed her to her toes. She was in such big trouble.

She tugged her hand free. "I'm doing fine." She blurted out the statement. "I just need to figure out what I want to be when I grow up."

"That's a hard one," he said.

She looked up, found him smiling at her, and smiled back. "Yeah," she said, picking up her spoon and attacking her cereal. "It is. I'm working on it. So far, all I know for certain is that I've retired from a life of crime. So the job has to be legit."

His mouth curved into a smile. "Probably a good primary criterion."

"In my family it's not one of those things you can take for granted."

He laughed, and she felt a little stab of pride.

"Yeah. I could see that," he said.

She aimed a smile at him and they sat in comfortable silence. After a while, he got up and put his bowl in the dishwasher. "Listen," he said, "we should probably get some sleep. Frances is usually up and ready for guests by about ten. You can have my bedroom. I'll take the couch."

She felt more disappointed than she cared to admit that he wasn't even going to try something. She was being foolish and she knew it, but, dammit, she was attracted to this man. And she knew he was attracted to her, too. And she really hated that he, apparently, had willpower. Because it was the middle of the night and she was tired, giddy and completely turned on. If she weren't so afraid of making a complete fool out of herself, she'd be making a pass at him right now.

Then again, maybe all of that was for the best. This was a one-night stint, and she really didn't need to wake up in the morning under a pile of morning-after regrets.

"I'm not going to kick you out of your bed," she finally said. "I'll stay on the couch. Besides, I really don't plan on sleeping. I'll just sit there and read."

"Afraid I'll skip out while you're snoring?"

"I don't snore," she said, once again irritated that he'd read her mind. "But otherwise, yeah. Exactly."

He nodded. "Fair enough. *I'm* going to sleep, so I'll take the bed. And you should sleep, too." He held up two fingers. "I promise I won't leave without you."

She wanted to trust him, really she did. But old habits and ingrained self-preservation instincts simply wouldn't let her. So instead of sleeping, she sat on the couch, flipping through magazines and trying to concentrate on the articles and not on the fantasies of Kyle Radley that filtered through her head.

KYLE WOKE UP ALONE and immediately wondered why he'd been so stupid as to go to bed that way. He'd spent the night lost in an erotic dream involving Grace's trim thighs and soft breasts, and he was absolutely certain that, had he simply made one move in her direction, he could have had the real thing instead of a dream.

No. That would have been a very bad idea. He'd called upon his willpower last night, and it had come through for him. He wasn't about to start second-guessing his instincts now. The woman might turn him on completely, but he knew trouble when he saw it. *Any* woman was trouble. A woman he'd caught breaking into Emily's bedroom was big-time trouble.

He'd keep his pants zipped and his head on straight and everything would be just fine.

The clock next to his bed flashed 6:10, and he groaned, his head pounding as he sat up in bed. He'd only been asleep for four hours, but he knew he was up for the duration. Trying for quiet, he headed into the kitchen to start some coffee.

As soon as the machine began brewing, he filled two mugs and headed into the living room. She'd said she was going to stay awake, and in that case, she was going to need coffee even worse than he did.

When he reached the couch, though, he couldn't help but smile. She was curled up on the sofa, half-buried under a maroon afghan he'd picked up in Tijuana one summer, hugging a throw pillow to her chest.

She looked completely at peace and absolutely beautiful, and he had to stifle the urge not to reach out and touch her, just to see if she was real.

He knew Frances wouldn't be up yet, so he might as well let her sleep. Quietly he made his way back to the kitchen, then got his briefcase off the small pine table he kept near the back door. He slid the file folders onto the kitchen table, and sat down to review the files and crunch the numbers.

He started with the balance sheets and immediately wished he hadn't. The business was okay for now, but unless they got some new clients soon, the company's meager profit would disappear. A typical scenario for a start-up business, he knew, but in this case, there were more than just market factors at work. As soon as Driskell ran off his mouth about the break-in, Kyle was screwed.

Driskell was being reasonable so far, yes, but who knew how long that would last?

He finished off his coffee, the caffeine already working its magic. He stood and grabbed a third cup, and on the way back, he fished yesterday's mail out of the side pocket of his briefcase.

A familiar logo caught his eye, and he plucked that envelope out of the pile. Modern Fidelity Life and Casualty. Driskell's insurance carrier. Shit.

Kyle had no idea why simply holding the envelope brought such a sense of dread, but it did. He ripped the thing open and extracted the letter, his fingers clenching tighter and tighter as he read.

Bastards. Those sleazy insurance bastards were trying to nail his company with Driskell's loss.

According to the letter, written by some smarmy company type with *esquire* after his name, Modern Fidelity was going to file a lawsuit seeking indemnification from Integrated, Kyle's company, on August 12. His eyes automatically drifted to the calendar. That gave him eight lousy days to figure out some way to save his company. Because once the lawsuit was filed, there was no turning back. The press would grab the story and Integrated and Kyle and his partner, Brent, would all be labeled incompetent.

The whole situation was a nightmare, and he balled the letter and tossed it across the room, then sat and stared at it until the businessman in him forced him to go recover it so he'd have it for the file.

He shoved it back into his briefcase and then

headed into the living room. He just wanted to see her. Just one glance to erase the bad taste of insurance and liability.

She was still sleeping, though she'd shifted a little, and now the pillow was on the floor. He watched her, then realized he was smiling. It had been a long time since he'd had a woman in his house. And this woman both enticed and intrigued him.

If he was a smart man, he probably would go on to Frances's house alone. Hell, if he left now, he could probably be back before Grace woke up. But he couldn't make a move in that direction. Like it or not, he'd gotten mixed up with this girl. She'd said she was his partner, and he had to admit he liked the sound of that. Not that he intended to admit it to her, of course.

She stirred, then peeled one eye open. After a few seconds the other eye followed, then her brow furrowed as she took in her surroundings. He could practically see her thoughts as reality returned and she remembered why she was there.

Slowly she sat up, the afghan tucked around her, even though she was fully dressed beneath it. "How long have you been up?"

"About an hour," he said.

"I fell asleep."

"I noticed."

"And you're still here. You didn't leave me."

He shrugged, kept his voice gruff. "Yeah, well, I said I wouldn't. So come on, already. Let's get this over with."

But that's when she smiled. And damned if his heart didn't melt just a little bit more.

4

"MORE ORANGE JUICE, GRACE?" Frances refilled her guest's glass even before the poor girl could answer the question, then went ahead and spooned out an additional serving of eggs. Apparently just in case Grace forgot that she was starving.

Kyle worked to hide his smile. From the moment he and Grace had walked through the door, Frances had assumed they were an item. He hadn't bothered to disabuse her of the notion, and so his aunt was going all out to make sure that Grace was welcomed into the family.

Any other woman might sink under the table and pray for sweet oblivion. Not Grace. She was holding her own with Frances, and Kyle wondered again if she was as much of a con artist as she was a thief.

The thought reminded him of why they were there, and he finished the last of his own juice—Frances hadn't bothered to refill his glass—and then put his napkin next to his plate.

Frances noticed the gesture. "Finished?" Her expression turned concerned. "You two aren't leaving already, are you? You just got here."

"Of course not," Kyle said. "We came to chat. After Grace met Emily last night she realized that meant that my aunt was *the* Frances Dormand, and she was dying to meet you."

"He'd originally told me your name was Frances McIntyre," Grace said. "It wasn't until I met Emily that I made the connection. You're one of my favorite character actresses, and, well, I begged Kyle to introduce me."

They'd come up with the story during the drive to the house. They didn't really need an excuse, of course, but considering that he was only supposed to be helping Grace to change a flat tire, they'd decided that it made the most sense to have some sort of story in place.

He could tell from Frances's expression that the plan was a good one. In a world where Emily tended to get all the attention, a little bit of fawning in Frances's direction went a long way.

"McIntyre's my married name," Frances said. "God rest his soul, Daniel was an old-fashioned man, and he wanted me to take his name and retire after we married. He was the chairman of a huge conglomerate, and appearances were important to him. I did, of course." She patted Grace's hand. "Those were different days back then."

Grace smiled. "I don't see anything wrong with that. Not if you made the choice out of love."

Once again, Frances beamed, and Kyle felt an absurd sense of pride. Ridiculous, since he wasn't really there to show Grace off to his aunt.

Deliberately, he pushed his chair back from the table and stood up. "I promised Grace I'd show her the upstairs den. And then maybe take her on a tour of the house. Is that okay?"

"Of course. Of course." Frances waved an arm in the general direction of the upstairs den. "All my old movie stills are hanging in that room."

"I can't wait to see them," Grace said. The plan was to get Frances in that room and then while she regaled Grace with stories of the past, Kyle would slip out and put the necklace back into the safe in her bedroom.

"You two go on ahead," Frances said. "My arthritis is acting up. I'll just stay down here and have coffee."

Kyle frowned. Frances hadn't complained about her knee in years. "Are you okay?"

"Of course, of course. Just wear and tear."

He wasn't entirely convinced, but he couldn't argue with good fortune. If Frances stayed downstairs, he and Grace wouldn't have to worry about sneaking away to replace the necklace. All in all, the situation couldn't have been better even if he'd planned it.

Grace caught his eye, and he half shrugged, then held out his hand to her. "Come on. I'll give you the nickel tour."

"I really would like to see the den," Grace said, as soon as they were out of earshot of Frances. "Frances wasn't ever as big as Emily, but she really is one of my favorites."

"I'm sure she'd appreciate knowing that," Kyle said. Frances's second-tier status had been at the heart of a long-standing family feud. Even her superior financial position after she'd married Daniel McIntyre hadn't mended the fences. Frances's biggest dream had been to win an Oscar, and Emily had never let her sister forget that she'd been the one to take them home. It was petty and stupid and, at this point, Kyle was pretty certain the feud was fueled more by habit than by any true ill will.

"Let's offload the necklace first," he said. "We can look at the den on our way back down."

As they headed for Frances's bedroom, he kept listening for footsteps, sure she'd change her mind and follow. But he heard nothing, and they ended up in her overly floral room all alone.

He shut the door behind him. "The safe's behind the Monet."

Grace squinted at the painting. "Is that real?"

"Far as I know."

"Wow."

He waited. She did nothing. "Grace. The painting."

"What?"

"The safe. Aren't you going to open it?"

She blinked at him. "Excuse me?"

"The necklace. Why we're here. Returning it, remember?"

"Well, yeah. I thought *you* were returning it."

He scowled. He had no idea what the combination was to Frances's safe. "Can't you just open it?"

She crossed her arms and tilted her head. "I appreciate the vote of confidence, but I don't have supersonic hearing and I didn't bring my stuff."

"You had it earlier."

"Yeah. It's in your car. I didn't realize I was on call. We can go get it if you want, but Frances is going to wonder what's going on."

"Fine. Okay." Actually, he didn't remember Emily taking the necklace out of the safe anyway. "We just need to leave it someplace where she'll notice it, but not realize that it just magically appeared."

"Like in a vanity drawer?" Grace crossed to the

antique vanity and pulled out one of the tiny drawers. Even from across the room, he could see that it was crammed full of cosmetics, hairbrushes, and various other girly things.

"Perfect." He pulled the box out of his jacket and opened it, then passed the necklace to her. "Just put it under a scarf or something. Not too hidden. We want her to find it."

"What if she doesn't?" Grace asked. "What if she just calls the cops and says it's been stolen?"

"I'll hear about it," Kyle said. "She'll either tell me, or I'll hear about it from my cop friends. I'll come over to have a look and—what do you know?—I'll accidentally run across it."

"That works," she said. She started to slide it into the drawer, but then she straightened, her perfectly white teeth worrying her lower lip.

"What?" His senses immediately went on alert. "Do you hear something?"

"No, no. It's just..." she said with a shake of her head. "I'm sorry. I'm just being silly."

Her cheeks bloomed pink, and he thought she looked completely adorable. He was also totally intrigued. "What?"

The color in her cheeks increased, and she spoke to her shoes when she answered. "It's just that my grandfather wanted me to have this necklace. Not that he had any right," she rushed to add. "But I've never seen anything so beautiful. And..." She gave a shrug. And when she looked up and met his eyes, he couldn't help but smile.

"Go ahead," he said. "Try it on."

"You're sure?" She licked her lips and made a face. "It sounds like such a girly-girl thing to want to do."

"It is."

At that, she rolled her eyes.

He just laughed. "I'm serious," he said. "If you want to play the princess, I'm all for it."

"Really?"

"Really." He moved up behind her and plucked the necklace from her fingers. She was facing the mirror, and their eyes met in the reflection. Without a word she reached back and pulled up her hair.

He draped the necklace into place, then fastened the clasp, his fingers brushing her neck as he maneuvered the complicated clasp. She shivered slightly, and he fought the urge to bend down and kiss her, ever so softly, right at her hairline. He was being sentimental and foolish, and those were instincts best left unexplored.

She let her hair fall free and then turned to face him. The necklace sparkled and shimmered in the overhead lighting. She'd changed out of her black turtleneck that morning, and now she wore one of his white button-downs. The top two buttons were unfastened, and the necklace filled the breach, fire and ice resting on a perfectly elegant Hepburnesque neck.

He wanted to run his finger over the fine bones there. To lean in and kiss the tiny indentations and smooth shadows. He stifled the urge, though, and instead simply told her that she looked absolutely beautiful.

MEL COULDN'T HELP the wide smile that crossed her face as his words still hung in the air. *You look absolutely beautiful.* "Any girl looks great in this many diamonds," she said.

"Maybe. But you look beyond great. You look on fire. And you definitely deserved to try them on."

She couldn't meet his eyes any longer. "Thanks. I really wasn't fishing for compliments. I just..." She shrugged. She couldn't explain it. And the truth was, she had a feeling he already understood. Heck, he seemed to be able to read her mind about everything else.

The truth was, the necklace seemed to call to her. She'd seen some amazing jewelry during her career, but this necklace took the cake. Warm and inviting, it had begged for her touch. And while she knew she couldn't keep it, that she had to give it up, she wanted just one moment. Just one tiny chance to play the princess.

Now that she had it on, she understood all the fuss about ostentatious jewelry. It weighed a ton, yes, but at the same time it seemed to hold her up higher.

She reached up, touching the stones at her neck. "They're so beautiful."

"Yes," he said from behind her. "You are."

She turned around, taking her eyes from her reflection to look at this man. The diamonds must be affecting more than her reflection, she thought, because right then all she wanted was to feel the touch of his hands on her body, the press of his lips against hers. She knew she was lost in the fantasy, but she didn't care. If she was playing the princess, then he was playing the prince, and she really and truly wanted to be swept away.

She took a step forward, her lips parted just slightly, her eyes never leaving his. His blue eyes darkened, like the sea at night, and he brushed her cheek, then traced his fingertip over the swell of her lower lip.

Her pulse increased, her whole body alive with anticipation. She wanted his touch, wanted his kiss, and she leaned in, ready to simply take what she hoped he would willingly give.

Their lips met, and his fingers twined through her hair. Her knees went weak, her legs unable to support her, and she was grateful for his other arm tight around her waist.

His mouth pressed hot against her, and he explored her thoroughly. Filling her and tormenting her. She wanted more but knew she couldn't have it. Not then. Likely not ever.

His hand stroked her hair, then caressed her neck, her back, before sliding down to cup her rear. He pulled her closer, pressing her tight to him, until his thigh was right between her legs and she could feel the hard length of him against her. The pressure of his body next to hers drove her wild, but she concentrated only on the kiss. On the way he tasted. On his masculine scent that overwhelmed her senses.

Dear Lord, he was driving her crazy.

He shifted then, and she realized he was leading her to the bed. Her head told her to protest. The rest of her followed willingly and begged for his touch. He eased her down, then straddled her, his knees on either side of her hips as he started to unfasten the buttons of her shirt. One button, two...

She drew a shaky breath, her stomach quivering as his fingers grazed her skin. He bent over, pressed a kiss just below her bra, and Mel was certain that she was going to come right then.

She tangled her fingers in his hair, wanting more. Wanting—

Below them the doorbell chimed, the sound echoing through the house and jolting Mel back to reality. She sat up, fastening her shirt as Kyle backed away.

She drew in a breath but couldn't meet his eyes. What the hell had they been thinking?

"Saved by the bell," he said, a slight tease in his voice.

She licked her lips. "Let's just get the necklace back in the vanity and get out of here before we—" She cut herself off. "Well, before we get sidetracked again."

"Good idea."

She stood up and readjusted her clothes, trying to ignore the lingering heat his touch had generated. She still wanted more, but she knew that was ridiculous. He didn't even know her real name, and as soon as this was over, she was heading back to her house and never looking back. That was the way it had to be. There might be some serious attraction brewing here, but she wasn't about to get involved with a guy who knew she'd been a thief. He'd never be able to respect her, and she didn't want to have to spend every day wondering if he trusted her.

She blinked, realizing she was getting way, way ahead of herself. They'd had only one kiss. He didn't even know her real name, he wasn't asking her out and she certainly didn't think he was making relationship plans.

Quit borrowing problems and get the hell out of there.

Right. Good plan.

She reached back and fumbled with the clasp. No luck. She tried again. Nothing. "It's stuck."

"Let me."

She turned and held up her hair so he could see the clasp. His fingers grazed her skin and she swallowed a moan.

"Sorry," he said, his voice low.

She bit her lower lip, not realizing she'd actually made a sound. "It's okay. I...um...laughed. Ticklish."

"Oh." He struggled with the clasp some more, his fingers doing a number on the back of her neck. Damn the man. Didn't he know the effect he had on her?

"Hold still."

"You're...still...tickling...me," she said, figuring a half-truth wasn't the same as a lie. His touch *did* tickle, but that wasn't the reason for her goose bumps and shivers. Holding her breath, she tried to take her mind off his fingers. Didn't work. All she could think about was turning around and losing herself in his arms again.

Bad plan. Very bad plan.

He'd cast a spell over her, some magic designed to fizzle away her common sense. She needed to get free, and so she jerked to the side, twisting away from him so that she could think clearly.

"Wait! It's—"

Too late she realized that the clasp had finally opened. She lost her balance and tumbled sideways, pulling him down until he landed with a thud on top of her.

Her first thought was that she'd like to stay right there on the floor forever. Her second, that she needed to get the heck out of there before proximity to Kyle fried her brain even more.

But then he shifted his weight, and her heart picked up tempo again, all rational thought evaporating. One of his hands pressed against her ribs, the edge of his finger grazing her breast.

Dear Lord, she was going to melt.

His breathing was as ragged as her own, and she could see heat in his eyes. He leaned forward, his lips parted, and she shivered, wanting him again, right then, right there, despite common sense and reason.

He paused, his mouth only inches from hers, and she could see the tension in his jaw, practically feel how tightly wound he was. "Shit." He ground out the curse, then rolled off her, using the vanity to pull himself up.

She stayed on the floor, not sure if she was relieved or disappointed.

He reached down and offered her his hand. "We need to get out of here," he said.

She nodded, not trusting her voice to speak. They slipped the necklace under one of Frances's scarves, then closed the vanity drawer.

She followed him out of the room and down the stairs. They would say their goodbyes to Frances and then head outside. The brisk sea air would restore her senses, and by the time Kyle dropped her at the bus stop near Miss Emily's house, she'd be her perfectly practical self again.

She told herself she couldn't wait.

But that, of course, was a big fat lie.

5

"DID YOU HEAR a word I said?"

Kyle forced his thoughts away from Grace and looked up at Brent Connors. His chief technician and right-hand man, Brent, was pacing in front of Kyle's desk. "What did you say?"

"I said money's tight enough as it is. We don't need a new assistant."

"It's not a point of discussion, Brent. If we want to keep this business growing, we need help."

Brent collapsed into the chair opposite Kyle's desk, then leaned back and put up his feet.

Kyle waved an irritated hand at the soles of Brent's loafers. "Do you mind?"

"Help? What are you talking about?"

"Running a business, Brent." His partner might own thirty percent of the business, but Kyle did one hundred percent of the day-to-day crap that kept the operation running. On top of that, he was the face man—the ex-cop who could get the clients, liaison with the community, and generally do the whole PR schtick while Brent designed and installed the systems. Having grown up at the edge of Emily's spotlight, Kyle was used to being on display. Brent, however, was a science nerd and was happy to be ensconced behind the scenes.

So far, the system had worked out great. And Kyle could see hefty profits in their future. But those profits hinged on getting out from under the Driskell mess.

Three days had passed since he'd dropped Grace off at the Laguna Beach bus stop, and, except for the occasional foray into fantasy, he'd spent the past thirty-six hours focusing on his business. But even that wasn't enough. Bills had been left by the wayside and calls gone unreturned. If he didn't want the business to go under even while he was trying to save it, he was simply going to have to buckle down and hire someone to help around the office. Because right then Kyle's priority was not only finding the flaw in Driskell's system but fixing it, as well. And for that he needed all of his resources—time, money and Brent.

"We'll figure it out," Brent said. His partner had a way of reading his mind that was both disconcerting and comforting. Brent had designed Driskell's system and done the installation personally. He was a total geek who took his job seriously, and he'd sworn to Kyle that the system was impenetrable. After the robbery, Brent had had to admit something had gone wrong.

"How?" Kyle asked. "How are we supposed to figure it out if we don't have any time to devote to the problem?" He picked up a pile of résumés the placement agency had sent over that morning. "No, I made up my mind last night. I'm hiring an office assistant. That's it. End of story."

Brent didn't respond. Instead he took a silver dollar out of his shirt pocket and started twirling it between his fingers.

Kyle shook his head, exasperated. Brent didn't want to deal with the situation, didn't want to admit his system was buggy, didn't want to admit that anything needed fixing. But it did, and Kyle needed his partner to focus. But focusing wasn't Brent's strong suit.

Brent tossed the coin into the air, and Kyle gave up and took the not-so-subtle hint. "Okay, okay. So tell me how you did at the tables."

"Up three grand. Not bad, eh?"

"Not bad," Kyle agreed. Too bad the money was in Brent's pocket and not the company's bank account. "So you're staying put for a while?"

Brent pocketed the coin and sat up straight. "Actually, I'm going back tomorrow."

Kyle closed his eyes and sighed. "Shit, Brent.

What have I just been saying? You know I need you here."

"You just need me to figure out the problem. And I think better in Vegas." He shrugged, and although it might have been a trick of the light, Kyle thought Brent actually blushed. "And, uh, well, I met a girl."

"The girl can wait, man. This is our livelihood I'm talking about."

"Come on, Kyle. You know I do my best work in the casinos. The noise inspires me."

"Forget it, Brent."

Brent scowled. "Can I at least work at home, or are you going to chain me to the office?"

Kyle held up his hands. "I gave up handcuffs when I quit the force. Home is fine. Just come in once or twice a day so we can touch base. See what kind of progress we're making."

"Fine. Whatever."

Kyle ran his fingers through his hair once again, thinking about his to-do list that just kept growing and growing. "And just so you know, this is exactly why I'm hiring an assistant. If I'm going to run this place solo, I need someone who can do the grunt work. So if you so much as hint that you're against hiring someone, I swear your slot machine arm will be in traction for months."

"Big talk," Brent said, his grin wide.

"Maybe," Kyle conceded. "But the sentiment's real."

Brent chuckled as he shifted in the chair. "So you were deep in thought when I got here. Thinking about anything in particular? Or anyone?"

Kyle looked up sharply. "Excuse me?"

"Ha!" Brent barked out a laugh and slapped his thigh. "I knew it. It's true." He webbed his hands behind his neck and leaned back. "So, what? How come I never heard of this gal? Did she get under your skin or what?"

Did she ever. "Yeah, she—" He stopped, stared at Brent. "How'd you hear?"

"Usual channels. My great-aunt's sister was at Miss Emily's party. And since she knows we work together, she asked me who your new girlfriend was. Imagine my embarrassment when I, your best friend and partner, couldn't give her any dirt."

"A tragedy, I know. But I don't have any dirt to give."

"No?"

"Sorry."

Brent unpeeled a stick of gum, popped it in his mouth, then leaned back again. "Well, at least give me something to work with. Who is she? Is she hot?"

"Yes, she's hot, and she's just a girl I met. She

needed help with her tire." Kyle had no idea why he was keeping the full story from Brent. Maybe because he figured Grace's secrets belonged to her and her alone. Or maybe he was just embarrassed that despite actually cruising by the bus stop on his way to the office every day, he'd been unable to find her again. He couldn't tell Brent who she was because he didn't know himself.

That little fact had been keeping him from sleep as much as his business worries had.

The electronic buzzer over the front door chimed, and Kyle stood up. "My first interview."

Brent rolled his eyes. "Have fun. I'm out of here."

But instead of a twenty-something looking for a job opportunity, Miss Emily swept in, passing Brent on his way out. She gave Kyle a quick kiss on the cheek and then took the seat Brent had just vacated.

He abandoned his desk for the seat next to her. She never ventured to his office—the traffic drove her crazy—and he couldn't help but be concerned. "Is something wrong?"

"No, no." She patted his hand, a little too casually, he thought. "Everything's fine. I was just at the bank and thought I'd stop in."

"And..."

She had the good grace to look a bit sheepish. "And I hadn't heard from you in a few days. I thought I'd see how you were doing. And Grace, too."

And there it was. He knew Emily wouldn't come by without an agenda, and he was relieved that it was a matchmaking one and not that she brought bad news.

"I haven't seen Grace in a few days," he said. He kept his voice matter-of-fact. He knew better than to let his tone even hint that he wanted to see the woman. If Emily got wind of the fact that he didn't know how to locate Grace, she'd have everyone from the Sheriff's Department to the Canadian Mounties pitching in to help.

Though, to be honest, there were times when he would appreciate the assistance. Because he did want to see her again. And it was taking a heck of a lot of willpower not to call in some favors with his cop buddies and see if they could track down a slim brunette with a record of cat burglary.

The frown lines at Emily's mouth deepened. "Did you two quarrel?"

He shook his head. "Nothing like that. I'm sorry if you got the wrong impression but the truth is we really didn't know each other that well." He thought of the kiss they'd shared and wished they'd known each other just a bit better. He cleared his throat, hoping the action would clear his brain, too. "I was just helping her out of a bind."

"I see." She stood, her handbag clutched near her chest as she started to pace the room.

He watched her for a moment, then broke down and asked, certain he'd regret it. "Is something wrong?"

"Oh, no." But her voice was a little too sing-song, so of course he didn't believe her. Besides, he knew exactly what was wrong. She'd assumed that he and Grace were an item and that her matchmaking days had come to a close. Now that she knew he was still on the market, he imagined her running through a mental Rolodex and wondered when she'd spring the next woman on him.

The possibility held even less appeal than usual, and he had to acknowledge the deep, dark truth—if any woman was going to be tossed into his life, he wanted the woman to be Grace. Foolish, considering he knew very little about the woman—with the very glaring exception of her felonious past—but there was no denying the impact she'd made on him.

"Résumés?"

He glanced up, startled back to attention, and saw his grandmother holding the sheath of papers.

"Yeah. I need an office assistant." He glanced at

his watch. "In fact, the first applicant should be here by now. The placement agency already has about ten interviews lined up for today."

"You're spending the whole day interviewing?"

"Yeah. Why? Are you applying for the job?"

He was making a joke, but Emily didn't seem to get it. Instead of laughing, she simply frowned. "Not me, of course. But an assistant. Hmm. Why, yes. Yes, I think that could work."

He studied her. "Grandma, what the hell are you talking about?"

"To help you out, I mean. You obviously need an assistant." She flashed him her most dazzling smile, then patted his cheek. "You do look overworked."

He couldn't argue with that.

"And now I simply must be going."

"You just got here."

"Errands," she said. "And you have your interviews." She paused in the doorway. "Good luck, dear. I'm sure you'll find the perfect woman."

And then she was gone. And Kyle was left with the distinct impression that she hadn't been talking about an office assistant at all.

MEL'S NOSE TWITCHED. That aroma, that smell. That delicious elixir.

She snuggled under the blanket, her hazy mind

forced to choose between the lingering dream of Kyle and the very real smell of coffee wafting around her.

Coffee? She hadn't set the coffeepot to brew.

She peeled her eyes open to the wonderful sight of a full mug swaying under her nose.

"'Allo, my dear. Sleep tight?"

She sat up and grabbed the mug from Gramps, sloshing drops of coffee onto her jammies as she greedily took her first gulp. She swallowed. *Ahhh.* She might survive the morning after all.

"Who are you today?"

He threw back his shoulders and smoothed his thin, gray mustache. "I'm Cary Grant. *To Catch a Thief.* Can't you tell?"

She clutched the mug tighter and searched his face for a clue that he knew about Kyle and his nick-name for her. Nothing, thank goodness. Probably just a coincidence that Gramps picked today to be Cary.

She took another sip. She didn't mind Gramps delivering coffee in bed. But she would have enjoyed another hour or two with Kyle twirling her around the dance floor in her dreams. She sighed. Three days had passed since he'd dropped her at the bus stop, and every night she'd lost herself in his arms.

Her dreams overflowed with Kyle, and when

Gramps had woken her, she still hadn't had her fill of him. Too bad, too, considering the only place she intended to see Kyle Radley again was in her dreams. No matter how much she liked him, no matter how much she craved him, there couldn't be anything between them. Not only did they come from two completely different worlds, but he knew her biggest secret. And rule number one was to never, ever get involved with anyone who knew she was or ever had been a thief.

Too bad. At twenty-five she was hardly a wallflower, but never once had she been out with a man who'd set her on fire all the way to her toes. And with nothing more than a look. When he'd actually touched her, she'd just about melted.

Kyle Radley was a walking, talking recipe for a good time. Too bad he couldn't be *her* good time.

She shook her head, trying to dissolve thoughts of Kyle along with the cotton in her brain. She took another slug of coffee. That helped. A little, anyway.

"So what are you doing here?" She'd told him that the necklace was safely back with Frances, and he seemed fine with that. Hopefully he wasn't here to announce the acquisition of yet another priceless birthday present.

"I'm getting you up, girl. What does it look like I'm doing?"

She raised an eyebrow. "You want to tell me why?"

"Betsy called. She's got some job she thinks you'd be perfect for."

"All right. I'll bite. Who's Betsy, and why is she finding me jobs?"

"A friend of a friend. Owns a placement agency in Los Angeles. I thought maybe she could help you out, and it looks like I was right."

"Really? That's great. Thanks."

"I'm supposed to make sure you get there by one." He aimed a disapproving glance toward her digital clock, clearly not impressed by her penchant for sleeping till noon.

Of course, he didn't know that she'd stayed up until three sending her résumé by e-mail to dozens of places she'd located on the Web. A long shot, but maybe she'd get a nibble.

A huge yawn sneaked up on her and she blinked a few more times, trying to wake up. Another hit of the coffee helped, and she let the warm liquid bring her slowly back to life.

She glanced over toward the clock, and reality filtered through her hazy brain. "There's no way I can make it in time." Too bad, too. She had no idea what sort of job this Betsy woman had lined up, but Mel was determined not to be picky.

"Nonsense. You've got plenty of time." He turned to her bookcase and grabbed a tall glass filled with something thick and green. "Here's your breakfast. Chock-full o' vitamins. Fixed it myself." He handed her the glass, then thumped his chest. "Not too tasty, but what a kick."

Her nose crinkled as she sniffed it. Somewhere between spinach and battery acid. "Um...I'm not really hungry."

"Fine, fine. More time to get ready." He waved his hand toward her closet. Her best suit was hanging on the back of the door. Really, the man had more energy than a two-year-old.

"All right. You win." She held out her mug. "Did you bring reinforcements?"

"Did Clark Gable give a damn?" He poured a refill from a thermos he'd left on her chest of drawers.

"Gable *didn't* give a damn, Gramps, so the answer would be no. But you *did* bring more coffee."

He cocked an eyebrow. "Did you understand what I meant?"

"Well, sure."

"Then hush up and respect your elders."

She grinned toward the floor. Nothing irritated Gramps more than getting caught messing up a movie quote.

She shuffled toward the bathroom, nibbling on

her thumbnail and considering Gramps's grand gesture. "So why the sudden foray into job placement? Did you finally realize that I'm never going to manage to find one on my own?"

She frowned at her reflection, then ran a brush through her hair. She'd showered the night before and slept on it wet. Perfect recipe for a bad hair day.

His heavy sigh seeped through the closed door. "I worry about you. And you're concerned about those taxes. I know. I see."

She grinned, positive there was more to it than that. "And?"

He cleared his throat. "And maybe I'm trying to hurry things along."

"What does *that* mean?"

"It means that until you've found a job and settled down, you won't be dating. And until you start dating you won't find a husband. And without a husband, I won't get great-grandchildren."

An image of Miss Emily's friends hovering over her and Kyle flashed in her mind. She opened the bathroom door and stuck her head out. "What is it with your generation, anyway? Haven't you got anything better to do than play matchmaker?"

"I'm old and feeble. Meddling in your love life keeps me occupied."

She ran her gaze over him. Sharp eyes, strong

shoulders, a thin, wiry body covered with a gray
sweat suit, and two-pound ankle weights on each
leg. Not a feeble bone or thought within a hundred
miles.

"Liar," she said, smiling.

"All right," he said. "So I'm not feeble. I still want
the great-grandchildren."

That she believed. The truth was, she wanted to
give them to him.

And it was exactly because she did want a family
that she needed to find a job on the right side of the
law. She needed to get moving on her new life. A
life where she could sweep the past away and start
over fresh. A life where, if someone asked her what
she did, she didn't have to lie.

She craved that life, would do anything to have it.
Even give up the thrill of her former life for it. She
had to, because the alternative was just too horrible.
True, Gramps did okay, but she'd seen the hurt in
his eyes when people shunned him because of his
reputation. In the Hollywood heyday, he'd been a
mystery, the dashing young extra who might or
might not have been "The Cat." But Hollywood had
changed, and so had the way people looked at
Gramps. Both the ones who knew and the ones who
only suspected.

Mel had heard all the stories and had seen

enough with her own eyes to know full well how a person's past could haunt them. How friends and family you believed knew you and loved you would suddenly shun you. Her own parents had refused to let Gramps see her. It had been an ironic twist of fate that had left him to raise her from the age of eleven after her parents had been killed in a car accident.

She wasn't going to let the same thing happen to her. Gramps had stayed in the game too long, and now he was a loner. Not Mel. She was already retired, and she was starting over. A new life. A new career. Her past was going to remain her secret. And she'd do what she had to, to keep it that way.

And the first step was to get a real job.

No matter how boring, tedious and monotonous it was.

THE WOMAN SITTING across from Kyle shifted, a bright smile plastered on her face as she clutched a fake leather portfolio in her lap. She was a bit gawky and awkward, but she seemed to know her stuff, and that was all he cared about.

He stole a glance at her résumé, trying to remember her name. "So, uh, Terri, why did you leave your last job?"

She licked her lips and didn't quite meet his eyes

when she answered. "My boyfriend and I, we moved to Irvine. And, well, I didn't want to make the commute all the way up to Burbank every day, so..." Her voice trailed off.

He nodded, then cleared his throat as he flipped through the file Betsy had sent over. Terri had been trained on all the basic office software and had a glowing recommendation from her former employer, the CEO of a small manufacturing company in the San Fernando Valley. She'd interacted with clients, answered phones, performed various secretarial functions. Basically everything that Kyle needed.

Except for the fact that carrying on a conversation with her was more painful than dredging up chitchat at a cocktail party, the woman really was perfect.

And it wasn't as if he actually *needed* someone in the office that he could talk with. True, it would just be the three of them, him and Brent and the new assistant, but he wasn't looking for a friend. He was looking for an efficient, competent employee.

He'd seen three girls that morning and had a fourth due at one o'clock. Not a huge sampling, he knew, but so far this one seemed to have all the basic skills even if she was painfully, awkwardly shy.

He asked her what kind of benefits and time off

she wanted, then flipped through the remaining résumés while she answered. Most of the applicants were lacking in some area, and he wondered if he should simply cancel their interviews. Only the one Betsy had faxed a few hours earlier looked as if it had potential. Melissa Tanner's overall qualifications looked great. Hopefully, she'd have some personality, too.

A chime sounded, a signal that someone had entered the reception area adjoining Kyle's office. Kyle sighed, then stood. "Excuse me for a moment," he said to Terri. "I think the next applicant is early."

He stepped into the reception area...and then stopped short.

There she was. The woman he'd scoured Laguna Beach for. The woman he'd spent three days fantasizing about. His Grace. Standing there all prim and proper in her conventional green suit, looking just as surprised as he felt.

He stepped forward, desperately afraid that she would bolt, then held out his hand in an attempt at bland professionalism. "Melissa Tanner, I presume? I'm Kyle Radley." He smiled. "How very nice to meet you."

6

MEL DIDN'T USUALLY find herself tongue-tied, but even she would be the first to admit that this wasn't the usual situation. Far from usual, it was instead both supremely fortuitous and supremely awkward. Awkward because she'd told herself that she really shouldn't see Kyle Radley again. Fortuitous because she'd been dying to do that very thing. No matter how much she wanted to deny it, she'd wanted to wrap herself in his arms just one more time.

And now here he was. Looking fabulous...and sexy...and, dear Lord, she was in trouble now.

She cleared her throat, trying for casual. "I, um, understand you have a job opening."

His eyes never left hers. "You're a hard woman to locate, Gracie Melissa Tanner."

"Yes, well, I—" She blinked, then stumbled over her own thoughts. "You were looking for me?" The knowledge sent a little trill of pleasure shooting down her spine and she stood up straighter.

"As a matter of fact, I was."

"Why?"

"Why do you think?"

The heat in his eyes gave the answer away, and she felt her cheeks burn. "Oh." She licked her lips. "Kyle, we can't...I mean, I can't..." Getting involved with this man would be a bad idea. She needed to keep reminding herself of that.

She lifted her chin, steeling her heart at the same time. "I need a job. That's why I'm here."

"A job. Right." He held up a finger. "Excuse me a second."

Mel watched, baffled, as he disappeared into the back room, then came out moments later with a woman at his side. He showed her to the door, promised to be in touch and then closed the door after her.

When he turned back to her, Mel raised an eyebrow. "My competition?"

"I've got a lot of interviews lined up today," he said, which only partly answered the question.

"I see." Mel crossed her arms over her chest, her pleasure at seeing Kyle dissipating as she remembered why she was there. A job. Property taxes. Food. All her other expenses and plans.

She wasn't a shoo-in no matter how much she wanted to be. For that matter, considering he knew her deep dark little secret, she wondered if maybe she shouldn't leave right then.

No. This was the best lead on a job she had, and she wasn't going to blow it.

Determined, she slid her résumé out of her thin leather briefcase, crossed to the receptionist desk, and dropped it onto the desk blotter. "I can type over a hundred words a minute, and I'm proficient in Excel, Word, Access..." She counted the programs off on her fingers. "Pretty much you name it. But I don't do dictation." She smiled at him, all bright and cheery. "Not really my thing." Of course, the truth was that *none* of it was her thing. But she was determined to get a job and to like it. "Well?" she prodded.

He didn't say anything, just leaned against the wall, his arms crossed over his chest.

Fine. He needed a little convincing. No problem.

She took a seat in the receptionist's chair, arranged her résumé neatly on the desk, then took two pens out of her purse and sat them alongside it. She picked up the phone, frowned at the odd configuration of buttons, then shook her head at him. "You really ought to upgrade. This system is ancient."

"I'll get right on that."

"Good." She clasped her hands on the desk in

front of her, church-and-steeple style. "Look, just hire me, okay? I know what I'm doing. You won't be disappointed." She felt a little pathetic begging for the job, but she was out of options. Unless she wanted Gramps and her out on the street, she was either going to convince Kyle to put her on the payroll or she was going to have to revert to her old career.

And *that* was something she'd promised herself she'd never do.

She was just gearing up for another round of pleading, when the front door opened and a tall, lanky man with fiery red hair and a smattering of freckles across his nose stepped into the room. He held a Taco Bell bag in one hand and looked much more like he belonged in a cornfield than an office.

"I thought you were working at home," Kyle said.

The man nodded. "Yeah, but I had to grab some stuff."

Kyle turned his attention back toward her, then nodded briefly in the other man's direction. "My partner, Brent." He gestured between the two of them. "Brent, Melissa. Known to her friends as Grace."

Considering the way Brent started to chuckle, she could only assume he'd heard their story.

He held out a hand, a broad grin stretched across his face. "Great to meet you, Melissa. I've heard a lot about you."

She shot a wry glance toward Kyle. "Yeah. I imagine you have."

"So where'd you two meet, anyway? And you actually got him to go out of his way to change a tire? I'm impressed. I didn't think he was that chivalrous."

Where did they meet? She turned her attention back to Kyle. So he hadn't told his friend she was a thief. Interesting.

She turned back to Brent, her smile wide. "Actually, Brent, he *is* that chivalrous. In fact, he was just about to save me once again by offering me a job."

Kyle glared, but she only smiled sweetly.

"Yeah?" Brent said. "Well, if he's going to insist we waste money on an assistant, then I guess a little eye candy is a good thing."

Kyle rubbed his temples. "Sorry," he said to her. "My partner is *not* the chivalrous type."

"Oh, come on," Brent said. "She knows I'm just kidding." He flashed a charming grin in Mel's direction. "Or maybe not. You really *are* one hell of a looker."

Mel blinked, not at all sure how to respond to that. "Um, thanks. I think."

Kyle just shook his head. "Go," he said. "Get your stuff and get out of here. I'm in the middle of an interview."

"I thought you'd already hired her," Brent said as he walked into one of the back offices.

Kyle's eyes never left hers as he answered. "Yeah, well, that remains to be seen."

Brent came back out holding a stack of file folders, a leather laptop case slung over one shoulder. "Well, I trust you to work it out. Melissa, Grace, whatever you go by, it was nice to meet you."

Brent was halfway out the door before she managed to say, "You, too. He's...interesting," she said to Kyle.

"He's brilliant," Kyle said. "And I've known him forever. He takes some getting used to, but I couldn't have built this business without him."

"Speaking of..." She licked her lips.

He shook his head, and her heart sank. "Sorry, Melissa. I can't do it."

"So much for chivalry," she mumbled.

He ran his fingers through his hair, then took a deep breath. "I'm sorry. I can't do it. I don't have a job for you."

She gestured around the room. "Typing. Filing. Phones." She leaned back in the chair and looked up at him. "I dunno. Sounds like a job to me."

"This is a security company. How would it look if I had a thief doing my filing?"

Mel flinched. There it was. The tone. The accusations. She'd never escape her past with people who knew her past. Hell, she should know better than to try. She should have turned around and run out the door the second she'd realized who he was.

She hadn't, though, because this was the only job on the horizon. And, damn it all, she still needed it. She drew in a breath, determined to convince him. "No one knows I'm a thief," she finally said.

"I do," he said.

"Yes, but you also know I'm retired. I told you so. And besides, if you're the only one who knows—"

"Can't do it. This company means too much to me. I can't risk the scandal."

"Kyle, come on. I don't see how—"

"Since I'm the one doing the hiring, it really doesn't matter how you see it. Does it?" He stared at her for a moment and then got up and moved back around the desk to the guest chair. The oak desk between them was only about two feet wide, but to Mel it seemed like an infinite chasm.

"I can't hire you for the assistant job, Melissa. I'm sorry."

"Call me Mel." She drew in a deep breath. "I...I

should probably go now." She stood up, gathering her things off the desk.

"Can I help?"

She tried not to sound bitchy when she answered. "Apparently not."

He frowned. "I could keep my eyes open for other jobs—"

"Believe me, I've been through the gamut." She patted her jacket pocket, checking for her car keys. "I'll be fine. I'm not your problem."

"Do you need a loan?"

Her temper flared. "No, I don't need a loan. I need a *job*. And I need it fast because frankly I'm all out of money and it's just—" She clamped her mouth shut, then squeezed her eyes closed. Damn it. She hadn't intended to do that in front of him.

She took a deep breath. Then another. When she felt calm enough, she headed for the door again. "Listen, thanks. I understand. I really do. No hard feelings, okay?" She pulled open the door and started to step outside.

"Wait!"

She stopped, turning to look back over her shoulder.

"I'm sorry about this. I really am. But it's just business. And I'd really like to see you again. Do you think we could do that?"

Every fiber in her body screamed yes, yes, *yes*. But her head and her mouth knew better, and instead of throwing herself into his arms, she simply shook her head. "No, Kyle. I...I don't think that would be a very good idea."

"You'd stay for the job." There was a note of accusation in his voice.

She met his eyes dead on. "Yes. I would."

His sigh sounded almost painful. "I'd like to help you. I really would. Against every bit of better judgment I'd actually like to give you a job. Hell, gainful employment would probably be a good thing." He flashed a teasing grin. "After all, I used to be a cop. I'm all for rehabilitation as a preventative for recidivism—"

Mel glared.

"— but the bottom line is that I have to protect my bottom line. My company is on shaky enough ground right now. I can't afford to have a thief working here. If word got around..." He let the words trail off, looking thoughtful.

She frowned. "Kyle?"

He held up a finger in a very Harrison Ford sort of gesture. Then he looked up, a huge smile crossing his face. "Sweetheart, I think I might have the answer to both our problems."

KYLE WANTED HER to say yes more than he probably should. And not because he could use her help clearing up the Driskell mess—though that was how he planned to convince her to stay—but simply because he wanted Melissa beside him.

"What?" She was looking at him with wide eyes, full of anticipation.

"Do you know anything about my company?"

Her brow furrowed. "Integrated Security Systems. One of the leading home security companies in Orange County. Owners Kyle Radley and Brent Connors. Sponsors a Little League team."

"Betsy fax you a cheat sheet?"

"Um, no, actually." She pointed to the Appreciation Award the company had received from the Little League organization. "I saw that on the wall. The rest I just assumed."

"So you don't know about our current crisis."

Her brow crinkled, and she shook her head just slightly.

He took some small comfort in the fact that his company's travails hadn't permeated the local news. "Well, the company's on shaky ground." He gave her the rundown, describing the Driskell break-in and his unsuccessful efforts to figure out the weakness in the system.

"I had no idea," she said with some surprise. "I haven't heard anything about it."

"And you'd know, I suppose."

She shrugged. "It's a small world."

He sighed. "Any idea about who it could be?"

She shook her head. "No. Doesn't sound local at all. Donovan's in jail. Carlysle died last year. And the new guys aren't any good. They'll just get caught in a year or so."

He stared at her, part amazed and part impressed. "You really know your stuff, don't you?"

For a second he didn't think she'd answer. Then she shrugged. "Yes, I do."

"Good, then you can test it for me," he said.

The confusion lingered, and then her eyes widened, lit with an emotion he'd felt many times or seen on Brent's face during a late-night session to fine-tune a system. *Excitement.* And the thrill of a challenge.

But as soon as he'd identified the look, it faded, her expression turning bland and unreadable. She shook her head, the small movement almost imperceptible. "I'm not a thief."

"I'm not looking for a thief. I'm looking for someone who can act like a thief and think like a thief. It's a temporary position," he added. "Just until I figure this mess out. But I promise it pays well."

She licked her lips, and he could practically see the wheels turning in her head. "You said you couldn't hire me."

"Not as an office assistant. But there's nothing underhanded about hiring a thief—sorry, a retired thief—as a thief. Everything will be completely aboveboard. Honest. Open."

"So you want to hire me to break into the Driskell place once you install the upgraded system?"

"To *try* to break in. And more, actually. I need your skills to assess the system that's already in place. Help me figure out the flaw and then test the upgrade once we install it." He spread his hands wide. "Of course, it's only a good plan if *you're* good," he said baiting her. "If you're just some two-bit burglar, you'll hardly be able to help me find the flaws."

"I'm good," she said, just as he'd expected she would. She licked her lips and moved across the office to stand right in front of him. She smelled delicious, and he wanted to sample and taste every last inch of her. Instead he just clenched his fists at his sides and tried to look like a professional. She eased closer, and though she wasn't touching him, she might as well have been.

"I don't know..." She worried on her lower lip. "I've given that up. I mean, I'm—"

"Looking for a job," he said, his voice calm and reasonable. Now that he'd thought of it, he was determined to win her agreement. "I'm offering you one. Security consultant. Completely legit. Completely aboveboard."

She nibbled on her thumbnail, doubt coloring her face.

"Come on, Melissa. What do you say?" Kyle asked. And then he held his breath and waited for her to either make or break his day.

MEL SAID YES.

Really, what other choice did she have? The job was too perfect. Too her. And, yes she'd given up burglary, but since Kyle had made it clear that no actual larceny would be involved, the position was a legitimate exception. Heck, it even had a cool title. "I've never been a security consultant before," she said. "Can I have business cards?"

He laughed. "I'll order them tomorrow."

"Good." Her smile matched his, and she realized she was genuinely excited about the job. And why not? Deep down in her heart of hearts, she missed the excitement of her old life. Missed doing something that she really and truly was good at. And she even missed the little thrill she got from knowing that what she was doing was not exactly on the right side of the law. It wasn't a life she could go back to, though. The risks were too great.

But *this* job, well, it was a real, honest-to-goodness, paying job. And for the first time in a long time she had a chance at real, successful, gainful employment.

"Thanks," she said, the word almost a whisper.

"I think I'm supposed to be thanking you. You're the one helping me out."

She shrugged. "Maybe we're helping each other. At any rate, I'm not sure why she did, but I'm glad Betsy sent me here today."

He smiled. "Me, too."

The air between them sizzled, and Mel fought the urge to step forward into his arms, to initiate a repeat performance of their kiss in Frances's bedroom.

For days, now, she'd been reliving that kiss, dreaming about it. Imagining Kyle's hands stroking her body and his lips pressed against hers. Now that she was here, though, standing right next to the man, she couldn't do it. Couldn't let herself get involved with him.

He knew her secrets, knew about her past. And that would never do. The whole reason she was looking for a legitimate job, the whole reason she'd walked away from the family business, was so that she could start over fresh. A clean slate.

She wanted a life where no one ever looked at her with suspicion. And that life wasn't with Kyle Radley.

She shook her head, frustrated with herself. Once again she was getting carried away.

She cleared her throat and fought the urge to nibble on her thumbnail. "So, um, where do we start?"

For just a moment she saw disappointment reflected in his eyes, but he shifted quickly enough to professionalism. Five minutes later they were at a small conference table, copies of the police reports relating to the break-in spread out between them.

"And now the insurance company is insisting that we're negligent," Kyle explained. "Their attorney has informed me they're going to file a suit for indemnification in six days." He pointed to a wall calendar, showing a big purple circle around August 12.

"So you want to prove it's not your fault."

"Basically," he agreed. "What I want to do is prove that the thief didn't just waltz in. That the system did its job, but that the burglar was extraordinary."

"To show that your company wasn't negligent," she said, thinking out loud, "that you didn't simply pawn off a sucky security system."

"Right."

"And if we can't prove that?"

"Then my business is going to tank."

"Well, so long as there's no pressure on me in my new job."

He met her grin, then rested his hand on top of hers. A simple gesture, it still sent sparks shooting all the way down to her toes.

She opened her mouth, not sure what she was going to say, but she never found out because the chime sounded in the reception area.

"Kyle?" Miss Emily's voice.

"Back here, Grandma," Kyle said, rising to his feet.

"Kyle, darling," she said, gliding into the room. Her gaze found Mel right away, and a smile bloomed on her face, her eyes dancing with such delight that Mel couldn't help but feel flattered.

"Grace! Darling, it's so good to see you."

"Thanks, Miss Emily," Mel said, standing up. "Actually, Grace is an, uh, nickname. My name's Melissa Tanner."

"Well, it's still a pleasure to see you again, my dear," Miss Emily said.

"Actually, Kyle and I are working together now."

"Fabulous." She clasped her hands and looked so delighted that Mel almost had to laugh. Apparently

Miss Emily was as much the matchmaker as her grandfather. Which reminded her...

"Miss Emily," she began, "it occurred to me that you know my grandfather. Gregory Tanner. He was a bit player in some of your movies. When I mentioned meeting you, he said that years ago you'd actually been acquainted."

For just a moment Emily looked quite befuddled. Then her face cleared and the perfect smile returned. "Gregory Tanner. Of course. I remember him well. A darling man."

"He seemed very fond of you, too."

"Gregory Tanner," Kyle said.

Mel turned his direction, curious about the musing tone of his voice. "Do you know him?"

"Only by reputation. Now I remember the story." He turned to his grandmother. "Gregory, The Cat. All those Hollywood stories about the dashing cat burglar. I used to read all about him in the boxes of fan magazines you kept in the attic."

"That's my grandfather," Mel confirmed. "Of course, his reputation was bigger than he was," she added with a meaningful look toward Kyle. "Certainly he was never proven to be a thief."

"Of course not," Kyle said. "Probably just a publicity stunt."

Mel turned back to Miss Emily and noticed that

her cheeks were bright red under the dots of already red rouge. "Yes," she said, "well, Kyle, I never realized you'd gone through all those magazines."

"My favorite thing to do when I was bored and you were off at some publicity thing. Lucy and I used to take a picnic lunch up there and spend hours. Great fun."

"Who's Lucy?" Mel asked.

"Funny you should mention her," Miss Emily said. "I'm here about Lucy."

"She's my cousin," Kyle said to Mel. He turned back to Emily. "Is anything wrong?"

"Quite the contrary," Emily said. "She's getting married. Frances and I are giving her an engagement party tomorrow night. Short notice, but her fiancé is in the military and is being called away for a short tour. I came to make sure you could come."

"Sounds great," Kyle said. "Where?"

"My house, tomorrow, eight."

"You couldn't have just used the phone?"

She waved a hand. "I've been running errands all day. I was in the neighborhood." She shifted a bit, pulling Mel back into this part of the conversation. "And it's a good thing I dropped by, too. Because, Mel, dear, I'd love for you to join us. And bring your grandfather, too. I know I'd so like to have the opportunity to catch up on old times."

"I..." Mel trailed off, wanting to accept, but not wanting to step on Kyle's toes.

"Say yes, Mel," he said, reaching over to squeeze her hand. "I promise I won't abandon you to the wolves this time."

Miss Emily's gaze drifted to their joined hands, and her smile broadened. "Good. Then it's all set. We'll see you two tomorrow and—"

"Grandma?"

"Yes?"

"Did you say you *and* Frances were throwing this party?"

Emily sniffed. "Of course, dear. Don't look so surprised. Lucy is my grandniece, after all. My sister and I may have our differences, but where the children are concerned, she and I can get along just fine." She tucked her purse under her arm and smiled. "Trust me."

7

KYLE POKED INSIDE the little paper carton with his chopsticks, trying to grab the last mushroom. They'd worked into the night, and now the office was officially closed. Not that you could tell from the conference table. It was littered with Chinese food containers, Diet Coke cans, file folders and paper.

Beside him, Mel was handling the chopsticks like a pro. She looked up with a grin. "Years of practice."

He gave up, snagged the mushroom with his fork and nodded at the papers. "See anything interesting?" It was just past seven, and they'd been working since Miss Emily had left about five hours earlier.

She shrugged. "It's all interesting. The question is still where to start." She blew out a noisy breath. "I wish Driskell would call you back."

So did Kyle. He'd left a message for the client about three hours ago. He'd been pressuring Driskell to set a date for Kyle to test and inspect the system, but the man had been in constant meetings and his assistant couldn't set a date without her boss's okay.

The delay was driving Kyle crazy, but at the moment, he had to admit he was enjoying the dinner break with Mel. "Thanks for working late," he said.

"Well, you know, we security consultants are a pretty committed bunch."

"So I've noticed." He reached out, smoothing his finger down her arm. She'd taken off her suit jacket and was now wearing a simple sleeveless top and a tailored skirt. She'd untucked the shirt and her pumps were in the corner of the room, next to the briefcase she'd dropped into a chair. She looked tousled and studious and sexy as hell.

He knew he should keep his hands to himself, but dammit, he didn't want to. He cupped the back of her hand in his palm, their fingers interlaced. She glanced sideways at him, a little smile on her mouth, and she didn't pull away.

"So this security consultant thing runs in your family," he said.

"It skips generations," she said, the hint of a laugh coloring her voice. "My father worked as a machinist. I take after my grandfather."

"What do your parents think about your choice of profession?" He watched her face, looking for a reaction. He knew he was prying, but he was curious. He tried to tell himself that he didn't often have the chance to chat with retired cat burglars, but it was more than that. He wanted to know Melissa Tanner. So help him, he wanted to know everything about her.

She didn't answer at first, and he feared he'd gone too far. Then she took a shaky breath and met his eyes, her own brimming with tears. "They were killed when I was eleven. And, no, they didn't approve of my grandfather."

He drew a breath. "I'm sorry."

"It's okay. I miss them, but that was a long time ago. And Gramps did everything he could for me."

"Even taught you a trade." It was a bad joke, but she didn't seem to mind.

"Yeah." She pulled her hand free to run her fingers through her hair, and he immediately felt a sense of loss. "The thing about Gramps is that he stayed in for all the wrong reasons. He started with petty theft back when he was just sixteen. He was trying to make ends meet while he worked to break into Hollywood. The cops couldn't figure it out, but there were stories leaked, and then suddenly Gramps had this whole persona." She shrugged. "I wasn't alive then, of course, but I think he got lost in the celebrity. He never made it big in the movies, but Gregory, The Cat, became legend."

"And he was never caught."

"Nope. When he got older, he retired." She shook her head. "I still can't believe he took the risk to steal that necklace from Emily."

"What about you?"

"I don't know. I guess it started as a crutch. Gramps had trained me and it was all I knew." She paused, and he stayed silent, not wanting to interrupt. "As I got older, I knew it was wrong. But by then Gramps had run through his savings and he really was too old to start climbing around on rooftops again."

"I guess there's no pension plan for those engaged in the cat burglary profession."

She laughed. "No. But that's okay. We take care of each other. I inherited my parents' house, so he's been living there with me, but I had to make enough to cover the taxes and our expenses, so I stayed with the family business." She shrugged. "I guess that's partly a lie. I loved the thrill, too. I knew I should give it up, but it was so hard. Finally, I just had to do it. I even went to college so I could figure out what I wanted to do with my life."

"What was your major?"

"History."

"And was that it?" he asked.

Her brow furrowed. "What?"

"What you wanted to do with your life."

She shook her head. "No. I'm still looking for that one. But it was a degree, and I figured it would help."

"But it hasn't."

She shrugged. "Yeah, well, I got one job right off the bat, but I got laid off a couple of months ago, and since the economy sucks, the job offers haven't exactly poured in." Her smile warmed him through and through. "But today I found a great job. And I'm determined. New life. New job. I'm starting over. I even—" She waved a hand, cutting herself off.

"What?"

"It'll sound silly."

"I promise I won't spread it around."

That drew a laugh, and she nodded. "It's one of my regular expenses. I treat it just like a bill. Like the electricity or water or whatever."

"Treat what?"

"Restitution." She practically whispered the word.

He shook his head. "I'm not following."

"I keep a list of all the names and addresses of people I've stolen from. And I have a little savings account. When the amount totals what I stole from someone, I get a money order and mail it to them anonymously. So far, I've paid back almost ten thousand dollars. And I'm determined to pay back every single dime."

He regarded her for a long moment, speechless with wonderment. "You will."

"Thanks." Her smile turned mischievous. "It'll be easier now that I've got a job, even if it is only a temp job."

He reached out and took her hand again, just wanting to touch her. "So you've found job satisfaction?"

She turned to face him, her mouth quirked up. "I think so."

"Maybe we should explore other kinds of satisfaction, as well."

Her breath hitched, and she dragged her teeth over her lower lip, the gesture supremely erotic. His blood heated, and he felt himself harden. The woman turned him on. No question about that. She craved the thrill of the job, but he craved the thrill of *her*.

He stroked her hand, tracing her fingers with a languid movement. She closed her eyes, her chest rising and falling as her breath quickened.

"Exactly what kind of satisfaction do you have in

mind?'' she asked, her tone laced with warm honey, though he doubted she was aware of the invitation in her voice.

He didn't say anything, just traced a path to her breast, then cupped the soft weight in his palm. He idly caressed her nipple, noting with pleasure how it hardened under his touch. Her breathing was ragged, and her lips parted ever so slightly.

''As much satisfaction as you can handle, sweetheart,'' he whispered. And right then he hoped she could handle a lot.

IT TOOK ALL of Mel's concentration simply to breathe. Common sense screamed for her to push away, to tell him in no uncertain terms that she was there only for the job. That they couldn't do this. That she couldn't allow his looks, his touch, his kisses.

She was turned on, though, and not just by his hands on her body. He did things to her, wonderful things, but it was more than that. It was the whole situation. She was going to be doing what she loved but without fear of recourse, and the anticipation tickled her senses.

She was trying so hard to keep him at arm's length. She'd been doing so well. And then Kyle Radley had gone and dragged her back in. Only this time, she owed him everything, because this job was allowed. This job was okay. And the truth was that the new job, the thrill of the chase, and the man himself all combined to throw her senses into overdrive.

She was on fire. She wanted this man. And she didn't have any earthly idea how to say no.

Why say no?

It didn't matter that Kyle knew her secrets, didn't matter because she knew she'd never have anything permanent with him. All that mattered was right then—that moment. She was worked up, tingling with desire. She craved him and he craved her and tomorrow could take care of itself.

Emboldened, she dropped her gaze, then with slow deliberation let her eyes drift upward over his jeans, over the telltale bulge at his crotch, and over the sexy white button-down that she so wanted to remove, all the way up to his eyes as she hoped to hell she wasn't blushing.

She leaned in a bit more, so that his palm pressed more firmly against her breast. "How much satisfaction?" she asked, throwing his question back at him. "I think I can handle whatever you want to give."

She'd hoped to knock him off balance with her careful inspection and bold words. But if he was wobbly, he hid it well. His eyes never wavered from her own, and that sexy grin that touched his lips was filled with one-hundred-percent male satisfaction.

She was wearing a sleeveless silk top, and he slipped his finger under the thin strap, then began to caress her shoulder, urging her closer as he did until she found herself wrapped in his arms, her rear end pressed against the edge of the conference table.

His hands were all over her, his breathing as ragged as her own. His hand slipped between their bodies to cup her sex, and she knew that she was already wet. She wanted him to yank her skirt up, to run his fingers over her panties and then inside the thin satin, to stroke her there. But she couldn't tell him that. The words seemed stuck in her throat.

"What do you want, Melissa?" he asked.

"You." She could manage only that one word, but it held a world of truth. She may not have planned this, but oh, how she wanted it. This man did things to her head, to her body, that no other man before ever did. She didn't care about tomorrow, didn't care that they'd wake up in the harsh light of reality instead of the warm glow of possibility. All she cared about was being in this man's arms. "I want you."

So desperately, in fact, that the power of her emotions scared her, all the more because this was not the Melissa Tanner she knew. That Melissa didn't believe in one-night stands. But for Kyle—no, for *her*—she wanted it.

Hell, she needed it.

He held her close, enveloped in those strong shoulders. That firm chest. Her nipples peaked under her top and she knew that even though this was a very bad idea, she was going to do it, anyway.

Slowly he inched her skirt up, his fingers caressing her bare thighs as he did. "Do you like that?"

She nodded against his shoulder, biting back the urge to demand that he hurry. He was taking his sweet time, and no matter how desperate her body was for his, she was determined to enjoy every single minute.

When her skirt was bunched up around her waist, he stepped back and let his gaze roam over her body, leaving her skin hot and needy in its wake.

"Soon," he whispered, and she felt herself blush. Her desire must be flashing like a big, red beacon. The realization should have reined her in, but it didn't. She did want him. Desperately. Hungrily. As she'd never wanted a man before.

She was certain he wanted her just as badly and she reached out, finding a boldness she'd never known before, to stroke the bulge in his jeans. "How soon?" she demanded, thoroughly satisfied when he closed his eyes and let out a slow, sensual groan.

He cupped his hand over hers, stilling her exploration. "Too soon," he said, "if you keep that up."

She smiled like a self-satisfied cat, but let her hand slip away. *Too soon* wouldn't do at all.

With a sweet smile touching her lips, she looked up at him, tried for demure and innocent and was sure she was failing miserably. "How bad do you want me there?"

He chuckled, a low, sensual noise. And then he stepped closer, until his hands were on her waist. He lifted her until she was sitting on the table rather than leaning against it. Without a word, he spread her legs and stepped inside the V made by her thighs. The soft area inside her legs pressed against the waistband of his jeans and, though there was nothing particularly erotic about the touch, it was all she could do not to slide forward on the table and grind herself against him.

He trailed his finger down her neck and between her breasts. Her nipples hardened and her mouth went dry. She desperately wanted him to kiss her, but she also wanted to see where he would lead them.

Lower and lower his finger traveled, ending up at

the rumple of linen skirt at her waist. "Oh no," he whispered. "Fair Melissa's clothes are amiss."

She lifted a brow. "'Fair Melissa'? What are you? A knight?"

He leaned in close and nibbled on her earlobe. "More like a Viking raider. I do plan on pillaging."

She swallowed. "Pillaging?"

"Absolutely." His fingers danced to her back, finding the button and zipper. She wriggled a little, helping as he tugged the skirt off completely. Her clothes were no longer just amiss, they were missing, and she wanted his the same way. She clutched at his shirt, her fingers finding the tiny buttons and undoing them one by one. When they were unfastened, he yanked the shirt off, dropping it to the floor.

He brushed his lips over her cheek, the stubble of his beard rough against her skin. His hands gripped her arms, pulling her close. "You're beautiful." His soft whisper brushed her ear, sending fireflies of desire skittering across her skin.

His words teased her senses, and she closed her eyes, losing herself to him as he pulled her close, his hand stroking her skin as they eased up her top. His thumb brushed the underside of her breast, and she shivered. "No bra," he said. "How lucky for me."

"I like to dress for seduction," she said. "Drives the men wild."

"It's certainly driving me wild." His hands slipped back down, his fingers gripping the hem of her shirt. He tugged it up and over her head as the cool air caressed her heated skin. He dropped her shirt onto the table. "*Now* you're dressed for seduction."

"I stand corrected," she murmured, tilting her head back just slightly as his lips brushed her neck.

He brushed a trail of kisses down her neck, then down between her breasts. His hands skimmed down until he was grazing her thighs with his hands. He bent lower then, and she gasped as he pressed soft kisses to her inner thighs, inching higher and higher until his mouth closed over her sex, a thin layer of satin the only barrier between her and the most intimate of kisses.

She pressed her palms flat against the table, her back arched, as he teased her with his tongue and his finger. He was taking her to the edge, closer and closer, and any moment now her body was going to explode. She moaned, her whole body tingling with wild sensations, and her sex throbbing with need.

He stood then, leaving her desperate and needy. His lips brushed hers, stifling her low moan of protest, before he littered kisses over her face, ending up at her ear and tugging gently on the lobe. "I want you," he said. And then, to prove it, he slipped his hand down between their bodies. His fingers slid under the nylon of her panties, his forefinger finding her slick heat.

"Tell me, Melissa," he whispered as he stroked her into a frenzy. "Tell me that you want me, too."

"I WANT YOU," she said, her palms cupping his behind. Her voice was soft, barely a murmur, but the fire in her eyes confirmed the words. As far as Kyle was concerned, they were the best words he'd heard in a long time. "I shouldn't, but I do."

He traced her jawline with the tip of his finger. "Why's that?"

Her breathing was ragged, and he watched as her areola puckered, all sweet and inviting. He wanted to taste her, but he wanted to listen to what she had to say, too.

She drew in another breath, but didn't answer. He paused midcaress. "Am I making it hard for you to think? Should I just stop?"

"Don't you dare."

"Then tell me."

"I'm...I'm the wrong sort of girl for you."

"Seems I'm the best judge of that." He knew what she meant, of course. Her family, her past. But he didn't care. She said she was retired, and he believed her. All that mattered to him now was the way she made him laugh and the way she felt in his arms.

She turned her head, a deep sadness underlying the passion in her eyes. "No illusions, right? We're just two people who are incredibly attracted to each other."

"Incredibly," he confirmed.

"This isn't...real." She licked her lips. "It's just sex."

It wasn't just sex to him. He didn't think anything could be just sex where Melissa was concerned. She opened his heart and that was something he couldn't deny. But he couldn't tell her that, not now. And the truth was, he had enough on his plate without trying to squeeze in a relationship. They needed time, and so he was willing to coddle her hesitation. At least for a little while.

"It *will* be sex," he said, forcing a grin, "if you'll shut up and let me get busy."

It worked. The haunted look in her eyes dimmed, leaving only the desire. A deep, burning desire that fired his senses.

Lord, how he wanted this woman.

"Then hurry up," she said. "Hurry up and kiss me."

She didn't have to ask twice. He wanted her, needed her, and he took the invitation, greedily pressing his lips to hers and drinking deep. Her lips parted, and their tongues met. It was raw and wild and utterly satisfying. A frenzied buildup of all the passion they'd kept buried. Lord knows he'd been on edge since the first moment he'd seen her.

He had to believe she felt the same way.

"Kyle." His name was a breathy whisper.

"Hmmm?"

"Get naked."

"Anything you want."

"I already told you," she said. "I want you. And I want you naked. And I want you inside me."

Her words shot straight to his penis, and he stiffened, fighting the urge to simply sink into her right then, right there. Instead he took five slow breaths and fought for control, then eased jeans and boxers off and kicked them aside.

"Better," she said. Her fingers teased him, one hand stroking his back, the other finding his hard shaft and stroking him there. He drew in a strangled breath. From the first moment he'd seen her, he'd wanted her, and now she was here. For now, at least, she was his.

He groaned, his entire body filling with pure, sexual need. He wanted to take it slow, to savor every touch, every moment. But as he stroked her bare flesh and watched the way her chest rose and fell, her breathing ragged, he knew that wasn't possible. He had to have her, and he had to have her now.

He claimed her with his mouth, and she leaned forward to meet him. Their mouths warred, tasting and demanding, full of heat and lust. He groaned, his entire body on fire, and he broke the kiss.

"I want to see you," he said, his voice gruff.

Her eyes were wide, her lips swollen, and she looked absolutely beautiful. "I'm right here," she whispered.

"So you are."

He stood back a bit, letting his gaze cover all of her, and rubbed his palms over her bare skin. Her breath came low and strangled, and he felt himself harden as he slipped his hands up to cup her breasts.

She writhed against him, her passionate, needy movements urging him on, calling to him, making him hotter than he could ever remember being.

"Please." Her voice was a strangled whisper.

He lowered his mouth to her breast, tasting her, laving her as she moaned beneath him. And then he raised himself, looking deep into her eyes. "Please, what?"

"Now. Dammit, Kyle, *now.*"

The need in her voice shot straight through him like a lightning bolt, setting his blood on fire. He burned with need, and right then all he needed was her. He had a condom in his wallet, and he bent down, fumbling for it. He slipped it on, then moved back in front of her, cradled in the sweet heaven between her thighs. He cupped her rear, lifting her up as he thrust against her, wanting to go slowly and gently, but she was so slick, so wet, that he thrust inside, needing all of her right then. She cried out "yes" and clutched his back, her fingers digging into his shoulders as they rocked together, a sensual dance that would lead them both to heaven.

Her soft moans increased, turning into little cries of passion, and with each sound she uttered, he came that much closer to the edge. Her tight, velvety heat stroked him, and he thrust again and again, claiming her, needing her, his entire body lost in a haze of passion.

The pressure built and built, and when he heard her needy moans turn to cries of satisfaction his release finally came, his body shattering into a million pieces. Then he collapsed against her, rolling her over until they both lay on the heavy oak conference table surrounded by leftovers and a shambles of paper.

She trailed her fingers up and down his back. "That was wonderful," she said.

He pressed a light kiss to her breast. "Yeah?"

"Yeah," she said, her voice soft and dreamy. "As a matter of fact, I think I'd like to do that again." She looked at him all wide-eyed and innocent. He had to grin. She wasn't innocent. Not at all.

And he was more than happy to comply with her request.

THEY SPENT TWO HOURS making love and by the time Mel settled back into the padded conference room chair to focus on the papers once again, she was thoroughly sated. She knew she should work, but she was curious about this man, and so she watched him, idly tapping the eraser of her pencil on the tabletop.

He looked up, his eyes bright with amusement. "If you can't concentrate, I can think of something else we can do."

"Tempting," she said, "but I think I need a little break."

"Girls," he said. "No stamina."

She tossed the pencil at him. "Okay, Mr. Macho Man. Tell me how you got into this security stuff in the first place."

He leaned back in his chair. "I guess it started

with my parents," he said. "They were diplomats, so we lived in embassies all over the world. I used to chat up all the security guys and military police and stuff. That was the only thing I liked about that life. The best times were coming here to spend a month or two with my grandmother."

"Where are your parents now?"

"Retired. Switzerland."

"Nice."

He nodded. "At any rate, I guess my childhood fascination rubbed off, because I wanted to be a cop." He flashed a mischievous grin. "Actually, I think I would have preferred your profession. The rush of adrenaline, the thrill of getting away with something. Except for that whole illegal thing, I'd say you had the perfect career."

"Yeah, that downside was unfortunate," she said, deadpan.

She could tell he was fighting a grin. "At any rate, I did the cop thing for about ten years, then realized that I hated reporting to someone else. I'd grown up pretty independently and I have trust fund money, so I quit the force and opened my own security business." He spread his hands wide to encompass the office. "The rest is history."

"You already told me you've been friends with Brent forever," she said, "but what about your other friends? Anybody I'm going to meet tomorrow night that I should know about? What about old girlfriends? Ex-wives?"

"My family's big, but my actual circle is pretty small," he said. "We moved so much, and then I've only been back in Orange County for a couple of years. As for wives..." He made a face. "Got close once. Didn't stick." He focused on her. "What about you?"

"Never even got close," she said. "And as for friends..." She shrugged. "It's hard to make really close friends when you have a huge secret hanging over you."

"It's not that bad a secret," he said. "I think a friend would understand."

"Maybe." She'd had some girlfriends in college, but had never pushed the point. It wasn't worth the risk. Wasn't worth seeing them look at her with disapproval in their eyes. "At any rate, it's not an issue now because I've gone straight. So no more secrets."

"Good for you."

"Right. Good for me." She licked her lips and focused on the papers in front of her, suddenly uncomfortable with the conversation. So far, at least, Kyle hadn't treated her any differently and *he* knew her secret. A tiny part of her wondered if maybe, just maybe, they could let this thing between them grow.

But she quashed the thought. She was being sentimental and foolish, letting good sex push out sound reasoning. She was here to do a job, and she needed to get busy.

Thirty minutes later, she was camped out in front of Brent's computer, a pad of paper in front of her and an Internet search engine pulled up on the screen. Her mind kept drifting back to their earlier encounter on the conference room table, and she pressed her legs together, fighting the urge to call Kyle over for the repeat performance she so desperately craved.

Determined to work, she paged through the hits, scribbling down suppliers for various bits of electronic equipment, the kind all the best burglars imported from Germany and Switzerland and utilized to circumvent state-of-the-art alarm systems. The equipment wasn't cheap, but it would do the job.

She hoped Kyle didn't balk at the cost—the tally was really adding up—but she doubted he would. The business was worth more to him than mere money. She suspected he'd pay to fix it out of his own pocket if necessary.

Across the room Kyle was tapping at his keyboard. From what she could tell, he was concentrating on work just fine. *Men.* Well, she wasn't about to be shown up. If he could focus, so could she.

"I think I got it," Kyle said.

"Got what?"

"Schematics to the Driskell system. Brent was re-organizing the network, but I think I found them. I'll print them for you."

She shook her head. "Don't bother."

His eyebrows lifted in question.

"You want me to penetrate the current Driskell system, right? See if we can find the flaw and then test whatever fix you and Brent come up with?"

"Right."

"And this is proprietary technology, yes? Not some system you bought at Wal-Mart?"

He didn't even bother to answer that.

"My point," she continued, "is that the thief didn't have the schematics, so I don't want them, ei-ther. At least not for round one. If I can't get in, then I'll take a look, see if I can find a weakness. But I want to make a go without the info first."

"Fair enough," he said.

"So, uh, you're getting a lot done, huh?"

"Guess so, under the circumstances."

"Circumstances?" she asked.

"Mostly I'm thinking about how I want to lay you across this desk and strip you naked."

"Oh." It was all she could do to force out a response. She tried to say something else, but couldn't even manage a sound. Their eyes met, and she started to melt under his heated gaze. Her thighs tingled, and she knew that she was getting wet from nothing more than the look in his eyes.

The phone rang, yanking Mel back to reality. She crossed and uncrossed her legs, her attention refocusing on the list on her desk. Across the room Kyle answered the phone, and Mel tuned out the conversation, lost in her own little erotic haze. When she heard Ethan Driskell's name, however, she banished fantasy and started to eavesdrop.

"I understand, Mr. Driskell. But finding the flaw will help us ensure that the upgrade is— Of course we're confident in our system. The tests are simply to help us ascertain the problem." Kyle ran his fingers through his hair. "Just a few days.... Well, that *is* understandable. When will you be back from vacation?... I see. Well, thank you. We'll be in touch to schedule the upgrade installation."

His face had hardened throughout the conversation, and as he hung up the phone, Mel was sure he was going to explode. She got up and crossed the room, settling herself on the desk in front of him.

He rested his palm on her thigh and looked up at her, a forced smile on his lips. "Hey."

"Hey, yourself. What was that all about?"

"Driskell's not going to give us access."

"Well, *that's* ridiculous. Doesn't he know we need to test the system?"

"Says he's going on vacation. Isn't comfortable with someone at his place while he's gone."

He ran his fingers through his hair again, a gesture she was beginning to find both familiar and endearing. "Hang on a sec."

He picked up the phone and dialed, then frowned. "It's me. Where the hell are you? Call me back as soon as you get this message."

"Brent?"

"Third message I've left today. Son of a bitch is supposed to be working at home."

"He's probably just too preoccupied to answer the phone." She scooted back onto the desk so that she could maneuver her foot onto his leg and press her toes against his inner thigh. "Want me to make you too preoccupied to worry about it?"

He closed his eyes and drew in a noisy breath as his hand closed over her toes. "Don't start something you're not willing to finish, Melissa. Right here. Hard desks. Hard floor. Personally, I'd planned on round three being on a mattress with sheets and pillows."

She urged her toes up higher, and was rewarded

with the hard length of him underneath her foot. "Don't be silly," she said. "We've already proved that a hard table works great. Why mess with perfection?"

She wasn't entirely sure how he managed it, but somehow now he was up and she was leaning back, her hands balanced on his desk. He was standing between her legs, and she locked her ankles behind him, then gave him a vixenlike grin. "All work and no play..."

He cupped the back of her neck, then kissed her, hard and demanding. Almost angry. She knew the anger wasn't at her, though. He was ticked at Driskell and he wanted her. Passion and need. A potent recipe.

She couldn't wait.

"Kyle. Please."

"Please, what?" But he didn't really need an answer. He knew. He stroked her thigh, his fingers sliding higher and higher. She drew in a breath and spread her legs just a little, silently urging him on. He took the hint, his fingers dancing around the edge of her panties.

"Wet," he said.

She nodded, unable to speak. Her entire body was throbbing, her nipples rock hard. She was already wet and ready, and she wanted him again.

"I like that." His hand cupped her sex, and she moaned, her hips gyrating as she tried to increase the contact between them, tried to get him to touch her just so, just *there*.

He slipped a finger underneath the elastic, then dipped inside her. She moaned, her body tightening around him, wanting him. "These keep getting in our way."

She nodded, wordless, as he knelt in front of her, his hands tugging her panties down as she lifted her hips, silently helping him. He stayed on his knees then, and pressed a kiss to the side of her knee. He had a hint of five-o'clock shadow, and the graze of his whiskers on her sensitive skin drove her wild.

He tugged up her skirt until his hands were at her hips and she was half-naked, exposed for him. It was wild and decadent and just like before. And, like before, she wanted his touch so badly she thought she would scream.

He seemed to know what she wanted, and his lips traveled up her leg, higher and higher as his hands held her hips still, keeping her instinctual writhing in check.

"Kyle." Her voice sounded hot and needy to her ears.

"Hush," he murmured, and she gasped as his

tongue slipped inside, finding her core and laving her, teasing her, bringing her right to the edge.

Oh, Lord.

She was close, so close, and he pressed further, his mouth working a magic on her as she arched her back, her body silently begging for him. The storm inside her grew and grew until she couldn't take it any longer. Then it burst, and she cried out, her body trembling from pure sensual satisfaction.

He stood and kissed her lips, and she collapsed against him, exhausted.

"Oh, Kyle."

He gathered her in his arms, pulling her onto his lap, holding her close. They stayed that way for an eternity, her body flowing back to normal, her need fading to the background until, finally, she could think again.

She was falling for him. Falling hard. So hard that she was having fantasies of happily ever after.

She cringed at the thought. That wasn't the future, and she shouldn't try to plan her life in a sexual haze. Help him, yes. Sleep with him, sure. Stay with him? *That* couldn't be.

With effort, she forced herself to think not about Kyle but about his problem. About Driskell and the theft and what the hell they were going to do. Her thoughts wandered, her face pressed against his neck as she breathed in the musky scent of sex and tried to concentrate on work.

"Kyle?"

"Hmm?" He stroked her hair, the gesture somehow more intimate than sex.

"What about another house?"

He moved, shifting her slightly so that he could look at her. "Another house?"

"If Driskell won't let you test his system, why not test another? Surely someone else has the same alarm system as Driskell. Maybe they'd agree to be our test case. It's in their interest, too, to work out the kinks." She cocked her head. "Or do you happen to have it at your place?"

"No. I've been so busy installing other people's systems that I haven't upgraded mine. But I like your idea."

"So there is somebody?"

"Three somebodies actually. One of them will be at the party tonight. I'll talk to him then." He shifted them both and then stood up as she hopped to her feet. He planted a swift kiss on the end of her nose. "Thanks for helping me out, Mel. It means a lot to me."

He squeezed her hand and she just about melted. She wanted to keep her distance, to put up walls by making some smart-aleck comment. But she didn't. She couldn't. And so she just squeezed right back and said, "I'm happy to help." Because that was the absolute truth.

8

"I'M SO GLAD you're coming, too, Grandpa," Mel said, her breath tickling the back of Kyle's ear as he maneuvered his Jeep past the gates that marked the entrance to Emerald Cliffs. She was sitting in the back seat, having deferred shotgun to her grandfather. She was leaning forward so that she could talk to both of them.

Gregory Tanner cleared his throat. "I'm still a little surprised Miss Emily invited me. We haven't...well, we haven't really seen much of each other these past few years."

"That's probably why she invited you," Kyle said. "To catch up on old times." He braked at a stop sign, then turned to face the older man. "I should probably warn you, though, that I think she's a bit enamored with your reputation. The Cat, I mean. Don't be surprised if she wants to hear all your stories."

"Not all of them, I hope," Gregory said. "Melissa told me how you two first met. I certainly don't

want to share *that* escapade with your grandmother.''

Kyle laughed. ''No, you've got a point. Probably
best to keep any stories you tell limited to the old
days.''

Gregory smiled. ''That I can do.''

Kyle met Mel's smile in the rearview mirror, her
gaze reflecting her thoughts—they hadn't told her
grandfather *everything*. Kyle had picked them up at
seven, easily finding Mel's house in Mission Viejo, a
more inland community about half an hour from his
house in Laguna Beach and a few million dollars
from Miss Emily's palace in Emerald Cliffs.

''Don't worry,'' Kyle said, as they got close to the
house. ''Mel or I will rescue you if Emily starts to be
too overbearing. She can be that way.''

''Yes,'' Gregory said. ''I know.'' He cleared his
throat. ''I mean, I remember.'' He smiled, his mustache curving with his lips. ''And thank you for
looking out for me. You're a good man. So nice of
you to bring me along on your date with Melissa.''

Kyle sneaked another peek at the rearview mir-
ror, this time to see Mel roll her eyes. ''I told you,
Gramps, it's not a date. I'm working for Kyle now.
Security consultant. It's a great job.''

She met his eyes in the mirror, hers dancing. He'd
brought business cards when he'd picked her up,

and the delight on her face as she'd run her fingers over the embossed type still amused him.

"Ah, yes. That's right. I thought perhaps you two were courting?" he said, turning the statement into a question.

"'Courting'?" Mel laughed. "Is it my imagination or did we just drive through a time portal?"

Gregory didn't say anything, and neither did Kyle. After a moment Mel sat back in her seat. "This isn't a date," she repeated. "And we're not courting."

And even though Kyle had known all along that she'd say that, he still felt disappointment kick him right in the gut.

WHAT THEY SAID ABOUT BRIDES was apparently true. Kyle's cousin Lucy glowed. No, more than that. If someone had cut the lights, Mel was certain that Lucy alone would illuminate the room.

It was a completely fabulous party, and Mel was clinging to Kyle for dear life. "I didn't realize there'd be so many people," she said. "Just how many relatives do you have?"

He frowned, then started counting on his fingers. "There're Emily's kids—my dad, his two sisters and his brother. They're all here, of course, except Mom and Dad." He gestured across the room to some people she'd met about a half hour earlier. She'd already forgotten their names and she told herself it didn't matter. She was here as Emily's guest and Kyle's employee, not because she was auditioning to be part of the family.

Kyle was still counting. "And, let's see, I'm an only child, but I don't think any of my cousins are, and there're five—no six—cousins. And then there're all of Frances's kids and Lucy's brothers and sisters and—"

She pressed her fingers to his mouth. "Never mind. I get the drift. Big family."

"I told you."

She sighed. "I know. I just didn't realize how big." Actually, it was kind of nice. She'd been expecting another Emily Radley Affair with a capital A, but this was more of a laid-back party. There were even toddlers—somehow related to Kyle, though she couldn't keep track of how—racing around the halls.

All in all it was loud and wild and, except for the fact that she couldn't remember anyone's name to save her life, she really was having a good time. "Your family's really nice," she said.

He smiled. "Yeah. They are. I hardly saw them when I was a kid—too much traveling—but they've always been around." He squeezed her hand. "I'm glad you're having a good time."

"I am," she said. And she meant it. "Gramps is, too." She nodded toward the couple in the corner. He and Emily were chatting like old friends over by the fireplace. "Guess they're catching up, huh?"

"I'm surprised they haven't kept in touch. Knowing my grandmother, Gregory is exactly the type of man she'd want in her life. She always did have an adventurous streak."

Mel shrugged. "I don't know. But it's nice they're together now." She took his hand, thrilled when he twined his fingers through hers. "I guess it's a good thing Gramps rushed me to that job interview. I'd never even worked with Betsy before."

"Rushed?"

"Mmm-hmm." She explained how he'd dragged her out of bed and got her moving.

"Betsy's the daughter of one of Emily's best friends," he said thoughtfully.

Something in his voice made her look up, and she noticed his expression, a mixture of curiosity and confusion.

"What?"

"Matchmaking," he said.

She shook her head, not following.

"I've been wondering why Emily suddenly quit

trying to fix me up with every woman in Orange County. She *didn't* quit. She just got sneakier."

"Kyle, you're not making sense."

But he was hardly paying attention to her now. "I know how to find out. Are you okay on your own for a few minutes?"

"Of course, but—"

She never got the question out. He planted a quick kiss on her cheek and then he was gone. Mel frowned, watching him go, then turned to find a waiter. Apparently, this evening required a glass of wine.

She snagged a glass of merlot, then headed in Lucy's direction, wanting to offer congratulations one more time to her and her fiancé, Jack.

"Thank you so much," Lucy said, after Mel found her. "And I'm so glad you came." She squeezed Mel's hand. "I'm even more happy that Kyle's found someone."

Mel's cheeks burned. "Oh, we're not—I mean, I just work for Kyle. We're just friends."

Lucy, however, looked dubious. And, honestly, Mel wasn't too convinced herself.

KYLE WAS HEADING for Frances when Jack caught up to him and gave him a hefty slap on the shoulder. "Congratulations, buddy. It feels nice, doesn't it?"

Kyle frowned. He didn't know Jack all that well, certainly not well enough to follow the man's train of thought. "What?"

"The ball and chain. Being off the market. Snubbing your nose at the singles scene."

"There's nothing going on between me and Melissa," he said, the words automatic because he knew that's what Melissa would want him to say. "She works for me. We're just friends."

"You are so full of bull."

Kyle couldn't help but laugh. He pointed to the beer in Jack's hand. "How many of those have you had, man?"

"Who knows? Who cares? I'm engaged. I love it. Should have done it years ago." A wide grin split his face. "Of course, your cousin's the only woman who could entice me, and I didn't know her years ago."

Kyle just shook his head. "Keep her happy."

"I will," Jack promised. "You do the same."

"I told you—"

But Jack cut him off with a wave of his hand, managing to splash beer on Kyle's suit in the process. "Come on, my friend. I can see it in your eyes. Hers, too. You guys are smitten with each other."

Kyle just stared, and Jack laughed, then slapped Kyle on the back one more time.

"Glad I'm not the only one head-over-heels for a woman." He lifted his beer. "To the girls," he said.

And because he didn't know what else to say, Kyle repeated the toast.

Jack took that as vindication. "Mel seems great," he said.

"She is." He said the answer without thinking, and he meant it completely. What the hell? Why not tell Jack how he felt? The man would be family soon.

They chatted for a few more minutes until Kyle noticed that Frances had moved away from two of his cousins and was heading toward the kitchen. He said goodbye to Jack and intercepted her just outside the room.

"What gives?" he said.

For just a fraction of an instant, comprehension showed on her face. Then her expression shifted, becoming blank and innocent. "I'm sorry, Kyle, honey, I don't know what you're talking about."

"Come on, Frances. Tell me the truth. Did Grandma and Gregory Tanner set Mel and me up?"

The color that rushed to her cheeks was answer enough. Kyle shook his head and rubbed his temples. "How?"

She explained the elaborate ruse to him, her voice barely a whisper as she went over the plans for the necklace and then explained how Emily had to call in the temp agency when it became apparent that he and Mel hadn't hooked up after Frances's house.

"Is the necklace even an heirloom?"

Frances shook her head. "Oh my, no. Emily bought it last month. It was my idea to add my initials. Don't you think that was a good touch?"

He grimaced. "The best."

She beamed.

He sighed. "Why didn't they just introduce us?"

Frances waved the question away. "Don't be foolish, my dear. Would you have stood still for yet another woman foisted on you by Emily?" She didn't bother to wait for an answer. "Of course not. This way was perfect."

"Except that we're not together."

"Pshaw. I've seen you two. You will be."

Kyle silently hoped she was right. And as he headed back into the party to find Mel, he realized that, this time, his grandmother really had played the matchmaking game perfectly. He'd fallen for Mel, all right.

Finally his grandmother had won.

"THEY SET US UP?" The party had finally wound down, and now they were in Kyle's Jeep, heading away from Mission Viejo after dropping Gregory back at the house. "It was all some sort of *scam?*"

"Yup. You've got to hand it to them, actually. It was a pretty intricate plot."

"I don't have to hand anything to them," Mel said. "I don't appreciate being manipulated."

Neither did Kyle as a rule, but in this case he had to admit he didn't mind too much.

They drove in silence for a while, him trying to remember the way to Doug Bryant's house and her seething in the passenger seat beside him. Bryant, a high-end client with a system nearly identical to Driskell's, had agreed to let his house be used as a test case. Since they didn't have time to spare, Mel and Kyle had decided that they'd do the initial run tonight.

"So they've known each other a lot better than they've let on," Mel said.

Kyle frowned, taking a minute to follow the conversation. "Yeah," he finally said. "I got the impression from Frances that Gregory and my grandmother were actually quite close. Probably would have gotten together if the head of the studio hadn't discouraged Emily from getting serious. Then your grandpa went and got married and—"

"And back in those days you didn't stay friends with someone you'd once had the hots for."

"Or still did have the hots for," Kyle added.

"You thought so, too?" She shifted in her seat to look at him more directly. "The way they were talking in the corner, I really got the impression that there were some serious sparks between them. And now that I know all of this..." She leaned forward, clearly excited. "Well, I think *they're* the ones who need a matchmaker. Not us."

"No kidding," he said.

"Let's do it."

He took his eyes off the road long enough to turn to her. "Do what?"

Her eyes were bright. "Turn the tables on them."

"You're kidding, right?"

She shook her head, color rising in her cheeks. She was eager and excited and completely beautiful, and her energy captivated him. "It's perfect. We'll pretend like we're dating. And then we'll arrange to do all these family things."

"Pretend we're dating," he repeated.

"Sure. They'll be thrown together over and over. Eventually they'll crack. I know they will. I saw how they were looking at each other at the party."

"Why not just *actually* date?"

She turned away, facing out the side window, her finger tapping on the window control. After a few minutes she lowered the window a tiny bit and the fresh, cool ocean air blew in. "No illusions, remember. No strings. No commitments." She turned to him. "You agreed. Remember?"

"I remember. Things can change."

"No. That's not what I'm looking for with you."

With you. Her words twisted in his gut. "Why?"

Her eyes darkened. "Because I want a fresh start. I need one. Hell, I deserve one. And you'll always see me as a thief. You know my secret, and there's no way around that."

"I'm not proposing marriage, Mel. I'm simply suggesting we date. See how this thing between us pans out. Because there *is* something between us, sweetheart. No matter how hard you try to deny it."

"I'm not denying it," she said. "I'm just saying we can't go there. I can't go there."

He fought the urge to bang his head against the steering wheel. The woman exasperated him. "How can you ever get involved with some other guy if you're going to keep secrets from him?"

"That's not your problem."

Her words hit him with the force of a punch, and he turned to face her. "Dammit, Mel, have I ever looked at you like you were a thief?"

She met his gaze dead-on. "Of course you have, Kyle. Or have you already forgotten why you wanted to hire me in the first place?"

And then, because she was absolutely right, Kyle couldn't do anything more than shut up and drive.

MEL CROUCHED in the shrubbery, her binoculars trained on the Bryant house as she tried not to think about dating Kyle or sleeping with Kyle or anything at all about Kyle. Unfortunately, he was sitting in a Jeep Grand Cherokee not twenty yards away, and even with that distance between them, she could still feel his presence and she sure as hell wanted to feel his touch.

By they time they'd traveled ten miles up the Pacific Coast Highway, the silence between them had dissipated and they'd agreed to turn the tables on their grandparents. Which meant that Mel was now officially dating Kyle Radley in a purely pretend sort of way. And it *was* only pretend. Mel had insisted on that, and in the end Kyle had caved. But even so, just knowing she was going to be spending all that up-close-and-personal time with Kyle made her body tingle.

She'd had to draw on deep wells of willpower to keep from jumping at his proposition to try dating for real. The man fired her senses. He was funny and kind and sexy as hell. If it wasn't for her—her past, her failings—she'd grab him tight and hold on for dear life. Lord knew she wanted to.

But she also knew that he'd never see her just as her, just Melissa. His perception would always be colored, and she simply couldn't live with that, no matter how hard she might be falling for the man.

She stifled a sigh, forcing herself to concentrate on the Bryant house. Time enough to think about Kyle after she did her job.

Mr. Bryant had readily agreed to help out Kyle, and the deal was that he had no idea when the break-in would happen. The next day, the next month. No clue. He'd given Kyle the code for his alarm system so that Kyle could arm and disarm as necessary. And Kyle had agreed that he or Melissa would inform Bryant when a break-in was under-way—*after* Melissa got inside—to reassure him that a real burglar wasn't at work.

They'd decided to do two runs. The first with the alarm system turned off, like a control group in a science experiment. That way, she could get a feel for how hard or easy the place was to get in when it was unprotected. Plus, she and Kyle could better gauge the strength of the protection once it was in place.

For each run, her mission was to get into the wall safe in the study and remove an item. Once she made a successful run with the alarm off, she'd turn around and do it again with the alarm on.

All in all it was nowhere near as useful as breaking into the Driskell mansion would be, but it was a close second. Plus, since Driskell had been adamant that no one break in while he was on vacation, they simply had no other option.

From Mel's perspective, it made little difference. It was the job itself that mattered, the job itself that fired her senses and made her tingle with anticipation—getting past the gate, getting past the locks and getting into a house she didn't own and where she simply didn't belong.

It was a familiar thrill. But it wasn't a thrill she should want anymore. And that disturbed her even more than her growing feelings for Kyle.

KYLE WATCHED FROM THE VAN as she moved slowly toward the Bryant house. The sun was dropping behind the foothills, and she seemed to dissolve in the shadows. His pulse beat in his throat. Even though they were doing nothing illegal, adrenaline still surged through him. Excitement filled the air, and he knew why someone would do this; why they'd take the risk. *The thrill.* Like skydiving or bungee jumping.

He shook his head, banishing such foolish thoughts. He wasn't here to get cheap thrills. He was here to try to save his business.

A few minutes passed as his eyes scanned the perimeter, trying to find any sign of her. No luck. He pressed the button on the microphone and whispered. "Mel? Melissa, do you copy?"

"Loud and clear." Her whispered tones filtered back through the speaker he'd set up on the dash.

"I lost visual. Where are you?"

"What do you mean where am I? I'm right where I'm supposed to be. In Bryant's library, staring at his wall safe."

He blinked, then looked at his watch. No way. He must have heard her wrong. "You're where?"

She laughed. "Don't sound so surprised, Radley. Did you forget why you hired me? I'm one of the best."

"You mean, you *were* among the best. Don't you keep telling me you're retired?"

"Right," she said. "*Was* the best. What are you, the verb police?"

He chuckled. "I'm not even the real police anymore, sweetheart. But if you can get into the safe just as fast as you got into the house, I promise I'll give you some sort of performance bonus when you get back out here."

"Oh, yeah? Like what?"

He made a show of lowering his voice. "Trust me, sweetheart. I'll make it worth your while."

Her laugh rang out over the speakers. "Mind out of the gutter, Radley," she said. He chuckled. His mind wasn't in the gutter. Hell, he almost wished it was. Gutter thoughts about Mel he could handle. But the thoughts he was thinking were hardly dirty. No, they were pure. Love. Commitment. Kids and family.

Scary thoughts for a bachelor, but for some reason these thoughts weren't scaring him at all. *That's* what scared him. Because *she* was convinced that she was the wrong woman. And Kyle wasn't sure what the hell he would do if he couldn't convince her otherwise.

9

MEL KNELT in front of the safe and studied it. Just as Kyle had said, a Sentronic 3000 with an electronic lock. Nearly impenetrable for an amateur, but, fortunately, she was no amateur.

She'd used the back of Kyle's SUV to change out of her dress and into black jeans, a black turtleneck and a black utility vest. Now she patted the vest, looking for the digital scanner she'd rescued from the stash of equipment in her Santa Ana storage room—all officially put away for good, of course.

She set it up, turned it on and went to work. Five seconds later the door to the safe swung open. She stepped back, grinning like a fiend. No doubt about it; she might be retired, but she still had the touch.

Not, she corrected herself, that she wanted the touch. She was simply making an empirical observation about her own skills. That's all. Nothing more.

Quickly she gathered her things and then made her way back outside the house. As soon as she cleared the residence, she hit the stopwatch button on her wristwatch and checked the readout. All told, it had taken her less than fifteen minutes to get from the Jeep, into the house, into the safe and back out.

Not too shabby for the control-group run. Now she just needed to make decent time with the real run. She was looking forward to the challenge, and right at the moment she was convinced she could do just about anything.

Thirty minutes later she wasn't feeling nearly as cocky.

Kyle had turned the alarm system back on, and they'd started the process all over again. So far Mel was still outside. She'd been trying to circumvent the alarm system using every trick she knew and a few she was inventing as she went along.

Nothing worked. Frankly, she was beginning to get ticked off. No, not beginning. She *was* ticked off. One hundred and ten percent.

She made another pass at the alarm controls, trying to shut down the system without tripping the alarm. The configuration, though, was unusual, beyond state-of-the-art, and Mel had to give Kyle and Brent Brownie points even while she cursed them.

She tried another approach, hoping to use radio

frequencies as camouflage for her movements. It was a relatively new approach to burglary, and she felt confident it would work.

It didn't.

Damn it all to hell.

"You inside yet?"

"Dammit, Kyle. Quit bothering me."

"Touchy, touchy."

She exhaled, then decided just to give it up. After an hour she knew she simply wasn't going to be making progress here. "Hold on. I'm coming back to the van."

Half an hour later they were in his living room and she was pacing the floor. He stepped in front of her and she stopped, hands on hips. "What?"

"Calm down. It'll be okay."

"You're not the one losing out on a performance bonus."

"True. But there is some good news. You told me you're the best, right? And you couldn't get in. So we know the system is sound."

"Not sound enough. Someone got in. There's a flaw, and I can't find it."

He rubbed his temples. "And if you can't find it, I can't fix it."

"The situation sucks, doesn't it? You were just being nice so I wouldn't feel bad for not being able to break in."

"Sorry."

"That's okay. I appreciate it." She did, too. Only once before had she not made it into a house that she'd been casing. But that was years ago, back when she was still a novice. This incident was downright embarrassing.

Or, rather, it would be if she was still interested in pursuing a career in the thieving arts. But she wasn't, of course.

She glanced over at him and caught him staring at the calendar. The days between now and August 12 were getting fewer and fewer.

"We'll figure it out," she said.

"We damn well better."

"I think our next step is for me to review the schematics."

He nodded. "They're on the computer. I'll print them out for you in the morning." He slammed his fist onto the coffee table, the unexpected movement making her jump. "Damn Brent. What the hell does he think he's doing just up and disappearing on me. The son of a bitch has left this hanging in my lap. He's the one who designed the system. He should be here trying to figure out the problem."

He drew in a breath and she sat down next to him, taking his hand. "I'm sorry," she said.

He exhaled, loud and long. "Don't be. I'm glad you're here. Hell, I don't know what I'd do without you."

"I haven't been that much help so far."

"Yeah," he said. "You have."

She smiled, her wounded pride at not being able to break in fading. They had to solve this riddle, true. But they weren't going to solve it tonight. And right now she wanted to see him smile.

She stepped back, then held out her hand for him. "Come on.

"Come where?"

"You'll see," she said. He stood and let her tug him into the kitchen.

Curiosity showed on his face, but he didn't ask, simply followed.

"Sit." She pointed to the table, and he pulled out a chair and sat.

And then, while he watched, she went to the freezer and pulled out the gallon of ice cream she'd left there the day before.

He just stared at her. "Ice cream?"

"Don't be absurd," she said. "I'm much classier than that." She opened the main part of the fridge and took out some toppings. "Ice cream with chocolate and strawberry sauce," she said.

His mouth curved just a bit, and she sensed victory. "What? No whipped cream?"

She reached in and pulled out a can. "Believe me, I've got plenty." She licked her lips, never letting her eyes leave his as she pitched her voice low. "Enough for ice cream...and anything else you might want to put it on."

That got his attention, and he watched as she carefully dished out perfectly formed balls, then drizzled chocolate over the top, garnishing the final product with a dash of strawberry goo. And then, of course, the whipped cream. She delivered it to him with flair.

"Voilà."

"Thanks."

She settled herself beside him and waited for him to take a bite. Instead, though, he slowly lifted up his spoon and fed her the first taste of his own sundae. It was a simple gesture, but somehow just as erotic as his earlier intimate touches. She let the ice cream melt in her mouth as she thought about this man. Kyle Radley. Prince Charming. He was perfect, and in the end, when she had to walk away, it was going to hurt like hell.

"What are you thinking about?" His eyes met hers, and she saw her desire reflected back.

"Whipped cream," she lied. "And you."

IF KYLE WERE A BIGGER MAN, he would have told her to take her no-strings arrangement and go jump in a lake.

But he wasn't that strong. He wanted Mel any way he could have her, and if that meant having her in his bed until she bolted, well then, so be it.

He knew she wanted him, too, with the same passionate ferocity that burned in his veins. And at least for as long as that craving filled their blood, then she was his.

He intended to make the most of it, and now they were sitting naked in his bed, a can of whipped cream between them.

"You really want to do this?" Her eyes were wide. "Your sheets—"

"Are washable." He took the bottle and squirted just a hint of cream onto her fingertip, then leaned over and sucked it off.

She laughed.

"What?"

"You are such a wimp," she said.

He pretended to be indignant. "Watch it, lady, or you'll be sleeping on the couch."

"Give me that thing." She held out her hand, demanding, and then, with a sultry little smile, she drew a line of whipped cream across her breasts. "Prove to me you're not a wimp."

That was a challenge he was more than happy to accept. He tossed her back onto the bed, his mouth closing over one breast. He teased and sucked until there was no more cream, just her nipple hard against his tongue and her soft moans sounding in his ear. He turned to her other breast and laved it clean, too. Then he sat up, smiled at her, and took the can away.

"My turn," he said.

She nodded, silent, then watched as he drew a white cream path between her breasts, over her belly button, all the way down to the dark triangle between her thighs. Then he settled in, licking and sucking his way down to his prize. She was hot and wet, and he was as hard as steel. He wanted her desperately, and he eased between her legs.

She shook her head, her lips parted, her eyes dark with desire. "Not yet," she said, reaching down to stroke him. "I haven't had dessert yet."

He almost lost it, but he held on to a shred of control. A shred that grew thinner and thinner as she ordered him to lie back, then smeared cream down the full length of his erection. His body was on fire, and from her sultry little grin, he was certain she knew exactly the effect she had on him.

When she lowered her mouth and licked the tip of him, he thought he heard himself cry out.

When she took him into her mouth, he knew he'd died and gone to heaven.

But when she licked the full length of him like a lollipop, he couldn't stand it anymore. He had to have her, and he rolled over, his body straddling hers, his breath hot and heavy, matching her own.

"Now," she whispered, and he didn't hesitate. Just slipped inside and drove home. Over and over and over until finally the world exploded around them and he collapsed, sated, against her.

They lay like that for a piece of eternity, until she made a little noise and moved.

"What?" he asked as a thick blanket of exhaustion fell over him.

She spooned against him, her breath caressing his neck. "Nothing," she said. "I'm just very, very glad that I saved room for dessert."

THE NEXT MORNING, they'd awakened before dawn and had arrived in the office before eight. They'd worked straight through, ordering lunch in and eating at their desks. And now Kyle watched as Mel rested her head in her hand. It was almost 7:00 p.m., and the schematics for the Driskell alarm system were spread out on the desk in front of her. She tossed her pencil down on top of them.

"Not going well?"

She shot him a nasty look. "I've got nothing," she said. "Absolutely nothing." She exhaled loudly. "What about you?"

"Not sure. I got the reports, but I need your help analyzing them." He'd called in a favor from some cops and had gotten police reports for every burglary within the last twelve months in the Orange County area. The reports filled his briefcase, and he needed her help going through them to look for any indications of a similar MO.

August 12 was bearing down, but the reports were portable, and the office was cramped and stuffy. Time for some fresh air and a new perspective.

She rearranged the stacks on her desk. "Just pass me a stack and put them here. I'll go through them right now."

"I've got a better idea," he said, then held out his hand. "Come on."

She twisted around to look at him. "Come where?"

"Out," he said simply. For a moment he thought she'd argue, and so he brought out the big guns. "We can take another spin in the convertible."

When they'd left together that morning for the office, he'd surprised her by opening his garage door to reveal a Mercedes convertible. A bright-red beauty.

Fifteen minutes later she was perched in the passenger seat, her hair loose in the breeze. She reached a hand up and caught it, twisting it into a knot and securing it with a clip.

"Want me to put the top up?"

"No, I don't want you to put the top up. But I do want to know where we're going. And why we're going anywhere with dozens of reports to review."

Kyle just grinned and shook his head. "I told you. A surprise."

"Uh-huh." A little grin played on her face, and he knew he was driving her nuts.

"Do you trust me?"

She licked her lips. "Should I trust you?"

"Hell no."

She laughed. "Well, I guess I'm just a naive little female, then, because, actually, I do."

"Wise woman. Astute. With amazing insight into the character of others."

"Uh-huh. Quit buttering me up and drive. I'm dying of curiosity over here."

"Aye-aye." He focused on the road while she leaned back in her seat, soaking up the setting sun and the sea-sprayed wind.

He cast a sideways look toward her. She looked

so beautiful, so happy. She'd inched her way into his life, and he was absolutely determined that she was going to stay. No two ways about it. He didn't care if she'd once been a thief, didn't care if that was some huge issue for her. They'd work it out. They had to because, dammit, he'd fallen in love.

He took a deep breath, concentrating on the road, as he let the simple truth into his head once more: he'd fallen in love.

This woman had filled his heart and his head, and he didn't intend to let her walk away.

Right now, though, he just wanted to be with her. Away from his family, away from the office, away from all his problems. Just him and Mel and the sand and the sea.

He turned onto Moss from Pacific Coast Highway and started looking for a parking place, actually lucking out and finding one near the stairs. He eased in, killed the engine and turned to Mel. "We're here."

She looked around. "Uh-huh."

"Trust me." The area wasn't much. Just a little neighborhood and a little street. But the beach below them was a treasure, and he intended to share it with her.

"I told you," she said, "I do."

The words were blithe, but spoken with such sincerity that they made his insides twist. He walked around the car, opened the door for her and then popped the tiny trunk and pulled out the cardboard box he'd shoved in earlier.

"Mailing a package?"

"Tru—"

"I know. Trust you."

He pressed a quick kiss to her lips. "Come on."

They headed down the street to the staircase that led to the small beach. He stole a glance back at her and was delighted to see the smile on her face when she saw the view. When they hit the sand, he took her hand and led her to a little nook among the rocks. He put the box down and opened it, pulling out a large blanket. He spread it on the ground and gestured for her to sit down. Amusement danced on her lips, but she didn't argue.

Next out of the box was their dinner. He'd ordered from his favorite restaurant, and the staff had packaged it up for a picnic. An entire smorgasbord of delights, and he laid them out on the blanket in front of them.

She plucked up a piece of baklava. "Wow."

"I brought the reports to review," he said, tossing the folders into the middle of the blanket. "But I thought we might be more productive if we worked through dinner, and then took a little time off to enjoy the show."

"Show?"

He gestured to the ocean. "Sunset," he said.

She took his hand and squeezed. "That sounds great."

He made a plate for her and they ate in silence until she turned to him, her eyes wide and wonderful. "Kyle, this is so special. What made you come up with this idea?" she asked.

There was a vulnerability in the question, and he answered it with a touch, pressing a kiss to the pad of his own thumb and then stroking it along her cheek.

"We've been working hard, and I thought we could use the break. And also because this has always been my favorite place to come and sit to watch the sunset. It's beautiful here." He shrugged, feeling a bit foolish and sentimental. "I wanted to share it with you."

Her eyes glistened, and she blinked, her teeth grazing her lower lip. Then she settled against him, her head on his shoulder. "Thank you," she said. "I don't think anyone's ever done anything so romantic for me."

He kissed the top of her head, unable to imagine that she didn't have men falling at her feet, wanting to make her feel loved and cherished. Because right then he knew without a shadow of a doubt that he would do anything, *anything,* to make this woman happy.

"I want you, Melissa." He'd said the words without thinking, and now he held his breath, feeling more vulnerable than he could ever remember.

"Kyle," she said, a teasing tone in her voice.

"No." He took her hands, waiting until she looked into his eyes. "I want *you.*"

She got it. He could tell by the tiny bit of terror that flashed in her eyes. "Kyle, I—"

"No. I don't care about your past. I care about our future. We're good together."

"Don't do this, Kyle," she begged. Tears brimmed in her eyes, and her expression cut his heart to shreds. "Please. You know how I feel."

Slowly he nodded. "All right, Mel. I won't do this tonight. But I *do* know how you feel. You've told me over and over. So now I'm telling you." He took a deep breath. "I want you, Mel. And I'm giving you fair warning. I know you think you can just walk away. Well, I don't. And I intend to do my damnedest to make you change your mind."

She didn't meet his eyes. "It won't work," she said.

"Yes," he said, "it will." He'd never been so sure

of anything in all his life. Because it had to work. Because the truth was, he didn't want to live without Melissa Tanner. He wanted her. She wanted him. And some way or another Kyle intended to make sure that they got each other.

THE NEXT DAY, Mel and Kyle finished the last of the reports, then headed over to Miss Emily's for lunch. It was a break they didn't really have time for, but they were doing this to further the Gramps-and-Emily plan, and so they'd decided to make the time.

Mel glanced at her watch. They'd already been there over an hour, and she was antsy to get back to work. The meal was slow going, though. Good, in that the molasses-like pace was the result of Gramps and Emily having a great time. Bad, in that time kept slipping away.

They'd started with salads and small talk. With the soup, Emily and Gramps had started reminiscing about the old days, laughing about various antics on the set. By the time dessert was served, the two grandparents wouldn't have even noticed if Kyle and Mel had spontaneously combusted right there at the table.

Mel caught Kyle's eye, then glanced meaningfully across the table toward Emily and Gramps. He nodded, his own smile amused.

They'd originally planned to meet at a restaurant for lunch, but Emily had hired a new cook and wanted the woman to get her feet wet. As it turned out, the decision was a good one. From the looks of it, Gramps and Emily weren't going to be moving from the table anytime soon.

Melissa dipped her fork into the chocolate cake, then brought it to her lips. "This is fabulous," she said.

"Thank you," Miss Emily said. "I'll pass your compliment along to the kitchen."

Mel smiled, then took Kyle's hand. The idea was for them to try to look like a happily dating couple, all the better to get their grandparents in the spirit of the thing. In truth, she wasn't sure either Gramps or Emily needed the encouragement, but since she was more than happy to hold Kyle's hand, she wasn't about to split hairs.

"Can I try a bite?" he asked.

She lifted an eyebrow. "You said you were passing on dessert."

"I changed my mind."

"Oh, sure," she said. "Make me give up some of my chocolate."

"The sacrifices you make once you enter the dating jungle."

She rolled her eyes, then chanced a glance toward

Emily and Gramps. Both looked delighted—in each other and in the banter between Mel and Kyle.

"Hey, come on," Kyle said. "I think I deserve at least a taste."

She fought a smile as she caught another morsel on the end of her fork and fed it to him. His lips closed over the tines, and she fought a little shudder, her mind conjuring images of those lips closing over her breasts and teasing her nipples.

Oh, Lord, what was with her? When she was with Kyle, even the most mundane actions seemed to raise thoughts of sex.

He licked his lips, and she fought another warm, gooey moment. "It's good."

She could only shake her head and laugh.

After a few more minutes she pushed back from the table and excused herself, giving Kyle a soft kick under the table. A message. Time for them to give the grandparents a little room.

She headed back to the small study near the front of the house to wait for Kyle. They'd already decided that they would disappear together for fifteen or twenty minutes. To give the grandparents a bit of alone time.

The room was lined with glass-fronted cabinets, each lit from within. They were filled with trophies and awards, and Mel eased forward, hoping to catch sight of an Oscar. Instead she found a collection of honors in Kyle's name.

Fascinated, she drew closer, like a moth to the flame. Here was Kyle's past, his triumphs and dreams, and she wanted to suck in the knowledge and hold it close inside her.

She stared into the first case, then realized she was hugging herself. God help her, she wanted to know everything. Wanted to know what made that man tick.

Wanted to know if his father had taken time away from playing the diplomat to toss Kyle a football. Wanted to know if his mother had cried when he'd become a cop, afraid her baby would give his life for someone else's.

She wanted to know all those things, but, damn it, she didn't *want* to want it.

She drew closer, drawn by the call of the gleaming trophies. They were all from college, which made sense, she supposed, since he'd traveled so much when he was younger. Debate Team, Most Valuable Member. She smiled. That one wasn't surprising; Kyle could argue with the best of them. State Chess Championship. Varsity Football. Track and Field.

The next case contained service plaques, also

from high school. Habitat for Humanity. Caritas. RIF volunteer.

The room painted a picture of an extraordinary man.

And right now—at this time and in this moment—that extraordinary man was hers. For once she really had gotten the prize...and she hadn't had to steal it.

For a long moment she stared at the trophy case, then realized she was shaking her head. She'd always been such a practical, pragmatic person. And yet here she was, lost in a life she was making up as she went along.

She closed her eyes and took a deep breath. She was living in a dream, and that wasn't a good place for a girl who'd been raised squarely in the harsh light of reality.

She wasn't Cinderella.

Kyle wasn't a prince.

And they weren't going to ride away into the moonlight. No matter how much she might wish they would.

"Quite the tribute, huh?" Kyle's voice behind her.

She turned and frowned, not sure what he meant.

He gestured toward the cases. "Most people keep that stuff packed up in the attic." He shrugged. "Emily likes memories. Mine and hers."

"I like your memories, too."

"Yeah?" He moved up behind her, wrapping his arms around her waist as she leaned against him, a solid male wall that wouldn't let her fall. Unreasonably, her eyes brimmed with tears, and she blinked them back.

"Yeah," she said. She snuggled closer, wrapping her arms around his. "How's it going out there?"

His mouth brushed her hair as he chuckled. "I think we've got ourselves a winner."

"Honestly?"

"Honestly, I think they're in love. Whether they'll admit it or not is anybody's guess."

Kind of like me. The thought came unbidden into Mel's head, and she clenched her teeth together, terrified she would say it aloud. She'd been avoiding thinking thoughts of love, of futures, of a life she couldn't have.

But she *did* love him, and she only hoped that she could walk away without tearing herself to shreds.

10

EMILY GESTURED to the waiter to clear their breakfast plates. Across the table, Gregory sipped a mimosa. They'd met here, at the little café overlooking the Pacific, to celebrate their victory in matchmaking. Of course, Gregory had ordered champagne—tempered with orange juice simply in deference to the early-morning hour.

She hadn't argued. She'd wanted to share this moment with him, even though she knew that their victory wasn't yet complete.

She took another sip of her own mimosa and sighed.

Gregory reached across the small table to brush his fingers over hers. "Emily? What's wrong?"

She forced a smile. "Not a thing, Gregory, darling. I'm simply watching the ocean and thinking about the passage of time."

That, in part, was true. So much time. She'd loved her husband, Clark, of course, just as Gregory had loved Martha. But they'd both been gone for years, and she and Gregory had wasted so much time.

She didn't want to waste any more.

"We were right, you know," Gregory said, still focusing on the children. "Mel's quite taken with Kyle." He rubbed his mustache. "As fast as they started dating, it should be no time before they're engaged."

Emily took a sip of her mimosa, stalling for time as she tried to decide how to answer. Their plan had definitely been a success so far, but she had to wonder if the victory was entirely legitimate. She'd tried to call Frances yesterday, but her sister had avoided her calls. That had been the usual state of affairs years ago, but lately they'd been getting along so much better.

Frances's hesitation had gotten Emily thinking, and she'd come to only one conclusion—Frances had slipped up. The woman had never been as good an actress as Emily. If Kyle had even an inkling of the strings the three of them had been pulling, he would have hounded Frances until she told him everything.

Which would explain why the children were suddenly so cozy. Their sneaky little grandchildren were trying to turn the tables on them!

In truth, though, Emily didn't mind. The only question was whether to tell Gregory. About that, though, she decided to keep her own counsel. Even more, she decided to do everything she could to move *both* schemes along.

"Emily?" he repeated, a hint of concern in his voice. "You do think it will work out, don't you?"

She studied him, thinking less about their own scheme and more about the grandchildren's. Finally she nodded. "Yes, darling," she said. "I think everything will work out perfectly."

MEL WAS CURLED UP on her sofa in ratty old sweatpants, a Robert Ludlum novel resting on the cushion beside her and *To Catch a Thief* playing in the background on the television. Gramps was in the armchair, his eyes glued to the screen despite having seen the movie at least a hundred times.

She'd been bummed when Kyle had told her he had to meet with clients that night, but now she was enjoying herself. She hadn't had the chance to spend much time alone with Gramps in the past few days, and she was looking forward to gracefully interrogating him about Emily.

"You and Kyle seem to have hit it off," Gramps said, keeping his eyes on the screen. Mel fought a smile, realizing that he'd jumped on the interrogation bandwagon.

"So have you and Emily."

His whole body seemed to come alive. He sat up

straighter, his eyes lit up and he seemed to lose ten years. She wondered if she looked that alive when she thought about Kyle, and promptly pushed the idea away. This was about Gramps. She already knew how her story with Kyle was going to end.

"Emily's a lovely woman," Gramps said.

She licked her lips, not sure how much to reveal, then decided she had nothing to lose. "I want the scoop. How come there wasn't anything between you two before now?"

He didn't answer at first, and she started to wonder if she'd crossed the line. Then he said, "Emily was already a huge star when I knew her, and I was playing bit parts. A character actor with a questionable reputation. That didn't stop us, though, and we went out a few times. I wanted more. I think she did, too, though she never specifically said so."

"What did she say?"

"She said no." He smoothed his thinning gray hair. "But the studio made her say that. Her persona was simply worth too much."

"What about later? Grandma passed away five years ago."

Gramps merely shrugged. "Where once we were young and foolish, now we're old and stupid."

She laughed and shook her head. "Foolish and

stupid. Okay. Got it. But are you still stupid? Or are you going to do something about it *now?*"

"Yes." He nodded, his face serious. "Yes, I am. Are you?"

She couldn't meet his eyes. "I know what you and Emily are doing, Gramps. And I appreciate it. I really do. But Kyle isn't the man for me."

"You don't need a clean slate, Melissa Jane. Not if the man truly loves you."

His words seemed to settle around her, but she pushed them away, not willing to hear them, certain that she was right. She kept her voice gentle yet firm. "I know what I'm doing, Gramps. Don't worry about me."

"I do worry about you. You're all I have."

She lifted a brow. "You have Emily."

His eyes lit up as he nodded. "Yes, I suppose I do." His mustache twitched as he smiled. "Apparently I'll be seeing her on a lot of double dates."

At that, Mel couldn't help but laugh.

The lines on Gramps's forehead crinkled. "What?"

She shook her head, still giggling. "Nothing. I just have that song going through my head now. 'It takes two, baby....'"

His mustache twitched. "Sorry. I don't do songs. Only movies. What about *Between One and Two?*"

"A silent movie? Nah. Maybe *Champagne for Two*."

Gramps shook his head, clearly getting into the game. *"Two for the Road."*

"Although, I guess really it should be four since we're two sets of two. So maybe—" She closed her mouth, her eyes wide as she realized that she knew. She *knew* how to answer the Driskell riddle.

Now she just had to prove she was right.

"I need a favor, Gramps," she said. "If you have any plans for tonight, I really need you to break them."

"YOU WANT TO TELL ME AGAIN what we're doing?" Gramps asked, stifling a yawn. "Considering you told me you were giving up this life, I know we can't be casing this house."

"That's exactly what we're doing," she said. "Of course, this time it's completely aboveboard."

Her grandfather's brows lifted.

"Trust me."

They were in her car, parked just outside of the Bryant house. If she was right, she knew how the Driskell robbery went down. She got a little thrill from having solved the mystery, but the excitement was tempered by the knowledge that, if she was right, the job she'd agreed to do for Kyle would be over. Time to move on. Time to walk away.

Tears threatened, but never appeared. She knew she was doing the right thing, no matter how hard it might be. No tears. She just had to buckle up and get past this.

It was a little past three in the morning, and the street lay silent. A fine mist of dew had settled over the car, and Mel hugged herself, pulling her hooded sweatshirt more tightly around her.

Gramps looked at her over his glasses, but didn't say anything.

She couldn't meet his eyes, so she concentrated on rummaging through her fanny pack, checking her supplies. The solution was so simple she couldn't believe she hadn't seen it before. After Gramps's casual words had planted the seed, she'd pulled out her copies of the schematics. Yup. Just as she'd thought. She now knew exactly, without a doubt, how the thief had gotten in.

"Okay," she said. "This is what we're doing."

After she walked him through the plan, he took off his glasses and peered at her. "And you think that will get us through the system?"

She nodded. "I'm sure of it."

"If you're right, you know what that means?"

She drew in a breath and nodded again. "I

know." If she was right, she was going to be delivering some seriously bad news to Kyle.

She opened the door to the van. "Let's go."

FOR THE THIRD TIME in the last three minutes, Kyle stopped pacing his office and glanced at his wristwatch. Ten-fifteen in the morning. And no sign of Mel.

He ran his fingers through his hair, frustrated. They'd spent the evening apart because he'd had dinner with clients, but the time away from her only accentuated how much he wanted to be with her.

He wanted her. Permanently. Forever. And as soon as they figured out this Driskell problem, Kyle intended to let Mel know in no uncertain terms that the time for playing games was over. She might not want a relationship, but he intended to fight her on that. He'd win, too.

His first priority, though, was Ethan Driskell and the damn insurance company. His gaze darted to the calendar. Time was almost up; the lawyers would serve him with a lawsuit the next day. He needed Mel in his life, yes, but he also needed her help.

So where the hell was she?

He was dialing her cell phone number for the third time when the chime sounded. He stepped into the reception area, expecting to see her. Instead, he saw Brent.

"Where the hell have you been?"

"Sorry," Brent said. "I had things to do."

"Things to do?" Kyle repeated. "I've been working my ass off."

"You said you were going to hire an office assistant."

"I ended up hiring a consultant instead."

"A consultant?" Brent asked. "What the hell for?"

"To do your job. Figure out how the breach occurred."

"Who'd you hire?"

"You met her. Melissa Tanner."

At that, Brent actually laughed. "Give me a break."

"She knows what she's doing. She used to be a thief."

"Really?" Brent frowned. "Well, I guess I wrote her off too quickly. More than just eye candy. The woman definitely has a more interesting side."

"You're on thin ice, buddy. Especially since she's the one who's been helping out while my partner— the man who actually *owns* an interest in this company—skipped out to Vegas."

Brent scowled. "I didn't leave town. I told you I wouldn't, and I stayed."

"I tried to reach you," Kyle said.

"I've been having a rough time of it, okay? I just needed—"

Kyle never found out what he needed because right then, the door opened and Mel walked in. Brent took the opportunity to step back into his office, and she watched him go, her face hard.

"Mel? Where have you been?"

She pulled her gaze away from Brent's office door to look at him, her mouth drawn into a tight line.

"What's happened?" Fear rose in his chest. "Are Emily and Gregory okay?"

"They're fine," Mel rushed to say. She drew a breath. "But you need to see this. Now." She passed him a file folder, her face completely unreadable.

Something in his gut twisted and he knew this was it. She was going to leave him. He wanted to call her on it, to beg her to stay, but the folder burned in his hand. He drew a breath and opened it, knowing it wasn't going to be good.

He skimmed the pages once, then read them in detail two more times. He knew in his gut that her report had to be right, but he didn't want to believe it. Finally he closed the folder and looked at her.

"I'm so sorry," she said.

"Brent and Driskell were working together?"

"An insurance scam," Melissa said. "I finally realized there had to be two people involved, and Gramps and I checked it out last night." She licked her lips, her eyes darting to Brent's office door. "It was an inside job. I finally realized it had to be. There was no way to get through the system. Not unless there were two people who were intimately familiar with the setup." She drew a breath. "I think you need to call the police in on this one."

"Shit." He ran his fingers through his hair. Her report would save him from the insurance sharks, yes, but it didn't save him from the knife of betrayal that Brent had wielded so skillfully.

He stormed to Brent's office and shoved the door open. Brent was at his desk, rummaging through the drawers. When he looked up, surprise and guilt flooded his face. "You son of a bitch," Kyle said, the words a growl in his throat. "How the hell could you do this to me?"

Mel was behind him, her hand on his shoulder, as if she was afraid he'd rush into the room and rip Brent's head off. Yeah, well, he just might do that.

"Do what?" Brent said, his eyes darting between Kyle and Mel.

Kyle tossed him the folder. Brent skimmed the pages, then looked up, all color drained from his face. "Who put this together?"

"I did," Mel said from behind him.

"Dammit, Kyle," Brent said, "you're going to believe *her*? I'm your partner, man. You said it yourself. She's a goddamn thief."

At that, Kyle lashed out, punching his partner in the jaw. Brent spun around, landing on his behind on the hard linoleum floor.

Behind him, Mel gasped, and Kyle turned to face her. "Sweetheart, I'm sorry about what he said. I'm—"

She held up a hand. "No. He's right. Just like you told him. I am a thief." She stood up straighter, her shoulders back and her chin high. "And I think it's time for me to go."

"MEL, STAY."

Kyle caught up with her at the front door, his hand reaching out to hold it closed. "Don't leave me now."

Brent was still on the floor in his office, even so, his words echoed in the air. *She's a goddamn thief.*

She steeled herself, sure she was doing the right thing. She *was* a thief. No matter what else she went on to do, that simple fact would always color her life. "I've made up my mind, Kyle. Please don't make this harder than it is."

"Don't make it hard? What do you expect? I'm sure as hell not going to make it easy."

"Kyle, please."

"Mel, we're good together. And *you're* good. Stay with me. Work for me." He waved the folder. "This is what you do. Don't walk away from it. Hell, don't walk away from me."

She shook her head. "I can't stay. You know how I feel. I never made any secret of it." She drew in a breath. She knew she was doing the right thing, but this was so much harder than she'd ever imagined. "And now I need to go."

"Dammit, Mel. I love you."

She flinched. She didn't want him to love her, and she didn't want to love him. But she did. And that made it so much harder.

"Stay," he said, his words filling the silence she'd left. "Stay and work for me." He cast a glance toward Brent's door, his jaw tightening with anger. "It looks like I'm in need of a new partner, anyway, and this is the perfect job for you."

"Perfect?" She felt a swell of anger build in her stomach. "You think a job where I break into houses is perfect for me? It's not perfect. It's exactly what I've been wanting to get away from. And if you think it's perfect, then you don't really know me at all."

"Maybe I know you even better than you know yourself."

His words held the force of a slap, and she flinched.

"You love it, Mel. The thrill. The challenge. And, yes, I know your past, but so what? It *is* your past. I love you anyway. You're trying so hard to be someone you're not. Quit trying. Just be yourself. Just be the woman I love."

His words stung, and she steeled herself against them. "I'm sorry, Kyle," she said, clenching her fists to keep her determination from wavering. "But you're wrong. It's not the job for me. Not at all." She took a breath, then met his eyes. "I do love you. But that really isn't enough."

KYLE HAD CALLED every few hours for the next two days, but Mel didn't take his calls. So far he hadn't come by her house, and she really hoped he wouldn't. She could steel herself against a phone call, but seeing him up close and personal would just hurt too damn much.

She knew she'd made the right decision, even so, she couldn't stop crying. God, she was such a mess.

With the back of her hand, she wiped her tears away, then returned to the laptop computer. She'd pulled up the Web sites of various placement agencies and now she scrolled through, trying to find a job—any job.

Her hand stilled over the mouse, and she closed her eyes. The truth was she'd had a great job. Kyle was right, the security consultant gig really was perfect for her. It challenged her and thrilled her. Besides, she was good at it.

No other job even came close in appeal, and yet she'd walked away, unable to face that her secret was out. That he'd shared her background with Brent. And worst of all, the reason he'd been able to spill the information was that he knew the truth about her.

She swallowed. He did know. And he still wanted her. Both in his life and in the job. Hell, he wanted her to be his security consultant *because* he knew she was good at it. And he knew she was good because he knew about her past.

Was that really so terrible?

She set her laptop aside, then pulled her spare pillow over and hugged it close. Her whole life she'd fantasized about finding a man who didn't know about her secret. Who thought she was perfect and loved her completely. She'd be a perfect princess; he'd be her Prince Charming.

But he would never really know her.

Kyle knew all her flaws and loved her anyway.

A tear fell, plopping onto the pillow, as if accentuating the truth. She'd made a huge mistake walking away.

A knock sounded at her door. "Come in," she called, her heart fluttering with the hope that maybe Kyle had come over, begging her to change her mind.

But when the bedroom door opened, it wasn't Kyle standing there, but Emily and Gramps. She couldn't help her smile. "Ganging up on me?"

"If it's necessary," Gramps said.

"Gramps, I—"

He held up a hand. "No. I want to say my piece, and then you can talk. Agreed?"

She nodded, fighting a smile. She glanced at Miss Emily, wondering if the elderly woman shared her amusement, but Emily was staring at Gramps with pure adoration.

"I'm in love with Emily," he said.

Beside him, Emily beamed, her hand clasped on Gramps's wrist.

"Oh, Gramps, that's wonderful." Mel scooted off the bed and kissed them each on the cheek, sure that she was beaming just as widely. "I'm so happy for you both."

"And *I'm* happy," Gramps said. He took her hand and squeezed. "I want you to be just as happy."

"I know. I really do."

"Don't misunderstand me," he went on. "I don't regret marrying your grandmother. But I never felt as alive with her as I do with Emily."

He gave Emily a kiss. "I missed out on years by not fighting for Emily. I don't want you to miss out, too."

She couldn't fight the bubble of laughter. "I won't, Gramps. I'd already made up my mind before you got here."

His face puckered in confusion, and then comprehension struck and the confusion faded, replaced by a broad smile.

"What are you going to do?" Gramps said.

She hugged him, then stood back, taking both their hands. "The only thing I can do. I'm going to tell him I was wrong. And I'm going to get him back."

KYLE TOSSED AND TURNED, trying to sleep. With the lawsuit no longer hanging over his head, he should have felt somewhat more relaxed. But Mel had walked out on him, and that had given him insomnia. Not only had he lost the girl, but now he was going to go crazy from lack of sleep. Hardly a fair trade.

He wanted to be mad at Mel. Wanted to call her

names and tell himself that the best thing that had ever happened to him was that she'd left him.

He couldn't, though. He didn't believe any of that. He loved her, and he'd lost her, and he didn't have a plan for getting her back.

He would figure it out, though. He'd been stuck at the office working with the police for the past two days, but he'd tried to call her every chance he got. She hadn't taken his calls, and he hadn't been able to camp out on her doorstep.

Tomorrow, though, was a different story. Brent was being arraigned in the morning, and after that, Kyle was going over to Mel's house, and he *was* going to talk to her. And if she wouldn't see him, he was going to talk to her grandfather.

Exhausted, he flipped over in bed again and lay there, his eyes closed as he soaked in the sounds of the house. Just breathing and relaxing. Doing absolutely nothing except wanting her and imagining that she was right there beside him.

"Kyle?"

Hell, he was even imagining her voice.

"Kyle?" A subtle pressure on the bed, and his heart swelled. She *was* right there beside him. He opened his eyes, smiled when he saw her sitting next to him.

"Do I need to grab you? Or are you going to run away from me?"

"I'm not running away," she said. "But I'd definitely like you to grab me."

He did, pulling her on top of him and then rolling them both over until they were lying in bed facing each other. He reached out, stroked her cheek. He wanted to savor this moment even as much as he wanted to cover her in kisses.

"Why are you here?" He almost didn't want to ask the question, too afraid he wouldn't get the answer he wanted.

She eased closer, her body pressing close to his. "Because I love you. And because I screwed up. And because I want to be with you if you don't want to kick me out."

He couldn't even answer her. Could only pull her close and cover her mouth with his. She was his. His love. His life. And she was right there in his arms.

Right there...?

He pulled back, fighting a smile as he looked down at her. "The chain's on the door and the alarm is armed. How'd you get in here, anyway?"

Her grin was wide and open. "How do you think?"

He lifted his brows. "I'm afraid to guess. The last

time I suggested that you might be skilled at breaking and entering, you walked out on me."

Her gaze dropped. "Sorry. I—"

He pressed a finger over her lips. "It doesn't matter. I love you," he said.

"I love you, too."

He folded her in his arms and held her there, the rhythm of her heart mixing with his own.

"Kyle?" Her lips were pressed against his neck, her voice soft, almost hesitant.

"Hmm?"

"I think I want that job. Is it still open?"

"For you? You bet."

"Kyle?"

"Hmm?"

"I want you, too."

He pushed back to see her face. Her eyes told him everything he needed to know. "Sweetheart," he said, "you've got me."

"Good." She sat up, smiling playfully. "And you better mean it. Because as you can see, I got into your house, and I can get into your life, too."

"You're already in."

"I know." She took his hand and held it tight. "And for the record, there's no way you're ever keeping me out."

"Is that a promise?"

She didn't answer with words, but her enthusiastic kiss assured him it was. And when she joined him under the covers, he knew that he'd found the woman for him...and that she really had stolen his heart.

_____Epilogue_____

MEL STOOD under the chandelier in Miss Emily's foyer, waiting for the wedding march to begin, her cue to walk down the aisle, exactly one year to the day after she'd first met Kyle Radley. She couldn't ask for a better birthday present.

Gramps stood beside her, looking dapper and happy. This was his foyer now, too, she reminded herself. He'd been living there for the past eleven months, the same length of time that he'd been married. A whirlwind courtship, yes, but, as Gramps had pointed out that, at their age, why risk a long one?

Besides, the wedding had been more than fifty years in the making. It had just taken some time for Emily and Gramps to pull it all together.

Mel said a silent thank-you that she herself had come to her senses, because she couldn't imagine waiting decades for Kyle. It had been hard enough waiting for the wedding after he'd proposed on the beach six months earlier.

She could hardly believe the day had finally arrived, and now here she was in her white gown, her veil and her blue garter, courtesy of Frances, to cover the "something old" requirement. Around her neck she wore a stunning diamond necklace, a wedding gift from Miss Emily, who'd wanted Mel to have the necklace that had brought her and Kyle together.

The music started and Gramps squeezed her hand. She gave him a quick kiss, and then they stepped through the doors and into the ballroom. From the far end of the room, Kyle smiled, looking absolutely perfect in his tuxedo. It was everything Mel could do not to defy the slow pace of the music and rush to his side.

Beside her, Gramps leaned over. "Nervous?" he whispered.

She shook her head. She wasn't nervous at all. Why should she be? She had everything she'd ever wanted. Somehow her dreams really had come true. Cinderella never had it so good. She'd only won that wuss Prince Charming. Mel had won Kyle Radley.

And in her book, that was worth a heck of a lot more.

...Michelle Reid

......Jane Porter

...Susan Stephens....

One Christmas Night

On sale 3rd December 2004

Available at most branches of WHSmith, Tesco, ASDA, Martins, Borders, Eason, Sainsbury's and all good paperback bookshops.

MILLS & BOON®

Volume 6
on sale from
3rd December
2004

Lynne
Graham
International Playboys
*The Winter
Bride*

FREE

2 BOOKS AND A SURPRISE GIFT!

We would like to take this opportunity to thank you for reading this Mills & Boon® book by offering you the chance to take TWO more specially selected titles from the Sensual Romance™ series absolutely FREE! We're also making this offer to introduce you to the benefits of the Reader Service™—

> ★ **FREE home delivery**
> ★ **FREE gifts and competitions**
> ★ **FREE monthly Newsletter**
> ★ **Books available before they're in the shops**
> ★ **Exclusive Reader Service offers**

Accepting these FREE books and gift places you under no obligation to buy; you may cancel at any time, even after receiving your free shipment. Simply complete your details below and return the entire page to the address below. You don't even need a stamp!

YES! Please send me 2 free Sensual Romance books and a surprise gift. I understand that unless you hear from me, I will receive 4 superb new titles every month for just £2.69 each, postage and packing free. I am under no obligation to purchase any books and may cancel my subscription at any time. The free books and gift will be mine to keep in any case.

T4ZEE

Ms/Mrs/Miss/Mr.................................Initials ....

BLOCK CAPITALS PLEASE

Surname ....

Address ....

....

....Postcode ....

Send this whole page to:
The Reader Service, FREEPOST CN81, Croydon, CR9 3WZ